Unmagic

Jane Glatt

The Mage Guild Trilogy

Unguilded
Unmagic
The Unmage

Unmagic

Jane Glatt

TYCHE BOOKS LTD.

Published by Tyche Books Ltd.
Calgary, Alberta, Canada
www.TycheBooks.com

Cover Art by Niken Anindita
Cover Layout by Lucia Starkey
Interior Layout by Ryah Deines
Editorial by M. L. D. Curelas

First Tyche Books Ltd Edition 2018
Print ISBN: 978-1-928025-84-9
Ebook ISBN: 978-1-928025-85-6

Author photograph: Eugene Choi
Echo1 Photography

This book was funded in part by a grant from the Alberta Media Fund.

Thanks as always to everyone at Tyche Books and especially Margaret Curelas.

Chapter One

"GYDA!" KARA SWORE. The knock on the door had startled her and the ball of mage mist she'd been controlling spun away and crashed into the bookshelf. A dislodged book toppled and hit the floor with a thud.

"We'll need to introduce distractions," Santos said as he rose and headed to the door. "We can't have you losing control of spells like that."

"Sorry," Kara replied. She got off the small stool and went to retrieve the book. In the month since her mother and Rorik had walked away from her, Santos, and Reo, she'd been desperately trying to learn how to manage her talent. Days like today, where she showed such little progress, were far too common. And that lack of progress was frustrating.

She had yet to clear spells from Warrior Guild's hall: every day that went by without that task completed increased her fear that Warrior Guild would demand Reo return to them.

Not that she'd seen Reo much in the past month. Their conversations seemed to always end up with him apologizing to her. As if he was to blame for every single terrible thing her mother had tried to do to her.

"It's for you," Santos said. "I'll go see what's going on in the kitchen."

Santos left and Chal Honess stepped through the door.

"Chal!" Kara hurried over and hugged him. "What a nice surprise."

"It's not just a visit, I'm afraid," Chal said. He looked her over, grinning. "But you look well. Are you happy?"

"Content," Kara replied. "I have a home and people I consider family." And if she still felt as though something was missing, well, it had only been a month since they'd all felt safe from Mage Guild. And Reo had moved in.

"Good." Chal placed his ebony hand on hers. "I'm glad. I too have a home; which I must return to."

"You're leaving Rillidi? When?" She pulled him further into the room and gestured for him to sit on Santos' chair while she took her usual perch on the stool.

"I sail tomorrow," Chal said. "Now that Reo is no longer in Warrior Guild, my services are no longer needed."

"I don't believe that," Kara said. Warrior Guild had always partnered with Seyoyans who could see magic, and now that they knew at least one person could also manipulate it, they were probably more interested than ever.

"Nor should you." He grinned. "But you'd be surprised how many people do believe it." He shrugged. "Another Assassin has tried to persuade me to stay but I've received word from home that my talents are required there."

"And you're not sad to leave," Kara said. She couldn't imagine Chal working with someone other than Reo.

"No," Chal agreed. "But I couldn't leave without saying goodbye. Or inviting you to come visit me in Seyoya any time you wish."

"I'd like that," Kara said. "I'll have to brush up on my Seyoyan first."

"Reo can help with that."

Kara frowned. "I'm not sure he'd be willing to: I think he's been avoiding me."

"Don't let him," Chal said.

"I'm not going to force my company on him when he's been very clear that he wants nothing to do with me." She tried to keep the bitterness out of her voice, but it was impossible. She'd thought she and Reo were . . . at the very least friends. And it hurt that he didn't seem to feel the same way.

"Kara." Chal leaned closer to her. "Reo isn't avoiding you

because he doesn't care; he's avoiding you because he cares more than he knows what to do with." He paused. "And he's ashamed of how he treated you and is furious with himself for putting you in danger."

"I know." She sighed. She'd told Reo that she didn't blame him; that she too was responsible for their desperate situation on Mage Guild Island. But he didn't seem able to forgive himself.

"He'll grow up," Chal said with a smirk. "Eventually. We all do."

"He's already a grown man," Kara replied. "He's years older than I am."

"But he has been free of his guild for less time than you have been free from yours," Chal said. "And that, being responsible for yourself, did that not make you grow up? Give him time."

"I guess," Kara said.

"I really must go," Chal said. He wrapped her in another hug before he sighed and stepped away. "I promise I'll visit next time I'm in Rillidi." Then he headed out the door and was gone.

Kara sat staring at the open door. She *had* grown up since she'd run away from Mage Guild. Maybe that was all Reo needed; time to grow up. Or time to decide what he wanted out of life. His goal had been to be free of his guild, but perhaps he'd never really thought he would be: perhaps he'd never thought beyond that point and now he wasn't sure what he wanted his life to be.

Kara sighed. And really, was she being fair? It wasn't as though she was sure what she wanted from Reo. Friendship, she thought, but they'd never actually been friends. They'd made a bargain and she'd spent time with him and Chal on Warrior Guild Island. But they hadn't been friends, especially not at the end when she'd defied him.

But they'd become close during their escape from her mother, and then he'd found Osten so she'd thought they were headed . . . somewhere. She sighed. She did know that this distance between them was awkward and frustrating. But was that because she wanted his friendship? Or because she wanted something more? And what did he want?

"You're ready," Santos said.

Kara was concentrating on her task so it took her a moment to understand what he meant.

"For Warrior Guild?" she asked. It was the only thing she'd been preparing for. When Santos nodded, she almost lost hold of the spell she was controlling. "You're doing this on purpose; trying to distract me."

"Yes," the Mage agreed. "I am. And since you passed this test, I believe that you truly are ready."

Kara pushed her hand into the spell, concentrating on making it disperse, watching as the grass-green mist lightened to white and then disappeared. "Are you sure I can do it?" She still had trouble determining if spells were malevolent. "I might miss a spell or two."

"Warrior Guild Primus Ungaro understands," Santos said. "I told him that you are a Journeyman, learning how to use your talent but that you are capable of doing some of what he needs done. Come along."

"Now?" Kara hurried after Santos as he left his workroom and headed down the hall towards the kitchen. She shrugged at Pilo, who was chopping vegetables, and followed the Mage outside, through the garden to the recently rebuilt pier that jutted into Pontus Bay.

She skidded to a stop, smoothing her hair, when she saw Reo standing stiffly on the pier. A small boat was tied up beside him.

"Are you ready, Reo?" Santos asked. The former Assassin nodded and moved aside to allow Santos to step past him and into the boat.

"Well?" Santos turned to her. "We don't have all day."

Averting her gaze from Reo, she hurried by him and scrambled into the boat. As soon as she'd settled in the prow she felt the boat shift as Reo got in. Santos waved a hand and green mage mist—a spell—surrounded the small boat and sent them skimming across the water.

Rather than look at Santos, and Reo behind him, Kara stared ahead, towards the walls that lined Warrior Guild Island.

She wrapped her arms around herself, trying to ward off the chill sea breeze. Santos could have warned her that she'd be out today; she would have brought a wrap or a cloak.

But then she would have spent the early part of the morning wracked with nerves, and not just because this was the first true test of her abilities. Reo's presence was a reminder that if she failed he could be sent back to a life he hated and worse, a life that would very likely be short and end badly.

So she wouldn't fail.

Kara closed her eyes and concentrated on making everything go away; all the doubts, all the worries, all the thoughts of how unready she was. She dismissed them all to concentrate on her goal: reading the magic and eliminating any spells that held any trace of ill will. She took a few deep breaths before opening her eyes.

Stone walls loomed straight ahead: they were here. The boat slowed as it approached a pier that stretched out into the bay. A couple of Warriors stood beside an older man whom she recognized from Founders Day as Guild Primus Ungaro.

Someone in their boat—Reo, probably—tossed a rope, and one of the Warriors caught it, pulling them close and tying their boat to an iron ring.

Kara put a hand on the wood of the pier and stood up, waiting until Santos had been helped from the boat before taking the hand offered by a Warrior.

"Santos Nimali," the older man said. "It is my pleasure to once again welcome you to Warrior Guild Island. Reo." He inclined his head towards the former Assassin, before meeting Kara's eyes. "And Kara Fonti. I remember seeing you at Founders Day, and I am especially happy to see you again. I am Warrior Guild Primus Ungaro. Come this way, please."

Santos took Kara's arm and leaned close to her ear. "You can do this," he said.

"Yes," she replied. "I can." She stayed focused as she walked into the hall, ignoring everything except the task at hand. And Reo, who followed her.

She looked around the large room. She'd been here only once, on Founders Day, when Reo had presented her to the Guild and she'd been seen by Noula.

There was even more mage mist here now but none of it seemed particularly ominous.

"Do you want all magic gone or just in certain areas?" she asked as she walked around, studying the spells. Ah, that one. "Although I will remove any spell that was cast by the previous Mage Guild Secundus." She frowned and waved a hand. After a moment, the grey-black cloud faded to nothing. "I assume that is acceptable?"

"I know from our Seyoyan friends that each mage has their own colour but I am surprised that you recognize the spells of Valerio Valendi," Ungaro said.

"I've seen his spells before. I've even seen him cast them," Kara replied. When the Mage Guild Secundus tried to kill her and Reo, but she didn't say that out loud.

She stopped scanning the room and stood eye to eye with Ungaro. "You know my mother is now Mage Guild Secundus?" At his nod, she continued, "I can identify her spells, in addition to those of her predecessor." Who was the father of her unborn half sibling, but she didn't say that out loud either. "And I have met—been threatened by—Mage Guild Primus Rorik."

"You have powerful enemies," Ungaro said. "As do I. I would appreciate it if you could eliminate spells cast by any of those three."

"Along with any others I get a sense of malice from," Kara agreed. "Shall you escort me?"

"Reo can take you," Ungaro said. "Along with Jacopo here." He gestured to a dark-haired man who stood near the door. "I would appreciate it if you could give me a report, once you're done." He turned to Reo. "And you wanted to view something in the Hall of Records, you said."

"Yes, Mage Primus," Reo replied. "There is a record there that Kara should see."

Curious, Kara looked over at Reo, but he avoided her gaze.

"You have my permission," Ungaro said. "When you're finished, Jacopo will bring you to me. I'll stay out of my office—and out of your way—for the rest of the morning." Ungaro nodded and strode out of the room.

Jacopo led them through hallways and into a series of office spaces for the next hour. There were quite a few spells, but none of them felt overwhelmingly dangerous. At least not that Kara could sense.

Until they came to the office of the Primus. It was blanketed in mage mist, some of which made Kara's skin itch. Surprisingly, it was Rorik's tan, not Valendi's grey-black or her mother's purple that felt the most threatening.

"Apparently Rorik doesn't trust Warrior Guild," she said as she started removing the spells. "Oh wait, there's a Valendi spell as well." The darker mage mist had a more sinister feel to it. She concentrated as she waved her hand over it: it faded to white before disappearing completely.

"It's not Warrior Guild that Rorik hates," Santos said. He stopped in the middle of the room and gazed around as though he too could see the spells. "It's Ungaro. He blames him for the death of his brother."

"Was he responsible?" Kara asked. Rorik's spells were easily cleared away. Was that because his magic was weaker than Valendi's or because at heart he wasn't as evil?

"In a way," Reo replied.

Kara glanced over at him. Other than explaining what went on in the rooms they were visiting, he'd been silent.

"Ungaro approved the contract." Reo shrugged. "It wasn't mine, but I know which Assassin fulfilled it."

"Rorik should blame whoever took out the contract," Kara said. "Shouldn't he?"

"Ungaro wouldn't let him see it," Reo replied. "Warrior Guild will assure confidentiality for those willing to pay for it."

"Otherwise the records are public?" Kara asked.

"Just within the guild," Santos said. "Any guild member who has found their talent or reaches the rank of Journeyman can view the records. Except records that are confidential. Usually only council members have access to those."

"And the record you think I should see?" Kara asked Reo. "Is that confidential?"

"No," he replied. "At least it wasn't when it was first commissioned. Come, if this room is clear, the Hall of Records is our final stop."

Reo led the way down a hallway to a set of double doors. He stepped aside to allow Jacopo to open the doors, before he stepped through the doorway.

Kara followed him into a huge room. She stared up at tall shelves. Books and scrolls and boxes lined the ones she could see, but higher up everything, including the ceiling, was obscured by writhing swathes of mage mist in every colour imaginable.

"And some of these records have spells of protection on them?" she asked. With her eyes skyward, she started walking along the shelves, one hand trailing along the wood. There—that must be it.

"Some do, yes," Jacopo replied. "I've been asked to tell you that those are to be left intact. Why?"

"Because I can see that Rorik has been sending spells to this record here." She reached up and pushed her hand into a thick rope of tan mage mist. She spread her fingers and the mist started to dissipate. "But I don't think he's been able to access it. The record itself is bound in a different colour of mage mist. Is this where the contract for his brother is?"

"Probably," Reo said. "But we are not authorized to see it." He paused and met her gaze. "But there is one we can see, if you want to."

"Yes," Kara said, although she already knew what it was: her mother's contract to assassinate her.

Reo studied the shelves as he walked along them, finally stopping and pulling a scroll from one. He unrolled the paper and glanced over it before handing it to her.

Kara stared at the paper in her hand. She'd thought it wouldn't hurt but it still did, even after all these weeks. Her own mother had wanted her dead—no doubt *still* wanted her dead.

She spread the paper so that she could read it. And quickly rolled it back up. It was a contract, written in dry language. There was nothing here that said why this contract was being created; none of the language spoke of the hate or anger that must have been behind this order; the words held no emotions at all. All it contained was the terms of the contract and her mother's agreement to pay upon proof of fulfillment.

"This should be guarded and preserved," Kara said as she ran her hand across the smooth paper. "Santos, can you do that?"

"Are you sure, Kara?" Santos asked. "Every time you come in here you will be reminded of what your mother tried to do. Is that what you want?"

She stared at the scroll before lifting her eyes to meet Reo's. His held sorrow and worry; for her. She sighed and looked over at Santos.

"Yes. I don't need to be reminded that my own mother wants me dead, but I will never let her pretend that she didn't do this; that she didn't order my death." And there would be a sibling who one day might need to know what their mother was capable of.

"All right," Santos said. He lifted his hand, and a stream of grass-green mage mist flowed up and over the scroll she still held.

"I've added a little spell to let me know if this is tampered with."

"Thank you." Kara handed the scroll to Reo, who placed it back on the shelf.

She stared up at the shelves, trying to distinguish the intent of the spells that writhed and swirled around them.

"Sorting through all these spells will take some time," she said. "And since some items here have had magic applied to them for good reason, I will only remove the spells that I am sure mean harm."

"Yes," Jacopo replied. "That is what Primus Ungaro wishes. This room, and any spells it contains, must be treated with caution. Not only are the records precious but the spells that protect them are valuable."

"In more ways than one, no doubt," Santos replied.

Kara nodded. With a Mage Guild Primus who had such a personal hatred of them, Warrior Guild could have trouble replacing any spells she removed by accident. And their confidence in any new spells they could buy would be very low, no matter what kind of contract was signed.

In the end she only removed four other spells, besides the one Rorik had sent. She was perhaps too cautious—she even left a spell that was Valerio Valendi's trademark grey-black—but she would be back next month, and the one after that. If her ability to read spells improved to the point where she could make subtle distinctions about the intentions of the spell, she could remove it then.

"I've done all I can today," Kara said.

Reo peeled away from the wall he'd been leaning against, and Santos stepped back from a window he'd been staring out of.

Jacopo, who had been trailing Kara, nodded.

"Then I will escort you back to Primus Ungaro," he said. He led the way to the door and waited while they filed out before shutting the door and locking it.

Jacopo motioned for them to follow him down a corridor.

"That was a very good start," Santos said as he fell in beside her.

"I feel like I should have done more," Kara said. "But I didn't want to make a mistake." She leaned closer. "Will it be enough?" She darted a glance at Reo, who was a pace behind them.

Santos sent a puzzled glance over his shoulder before shaking his head. "That has already been settled, you know that. Reo is not returning to Warrior Guild."

"Are you sure? I thought that if I didn't—"

"Kara," Santos said. "It is done." He sighed. "I should have shown you *that* contract while we were in the Hall of Records. The terms are unequivocal. Reo is free from Warrior Guild. In return, I and my Apprentice will—exclusively and to the best of our abilities—keep Warrior Guild free from spells that seek to harm them. They do not have the right to terminate the contract as long as we work to the best of our abilities."

"Oh." She paused. "That doesn't seem like a very good bargain for them. What if I couldn't do anything?"

"It was a risk Primus Ungaro was willing to take," Santos said. "What is the loss of one Assassin against the potential to even partially ensure the safety and integrity of his hall? His key request was exclusivity. He does not want us performing the same service for any other guild."

Jacopo knocked on a door before opening it. "Warrior Guild Primus Ungaro," he said as he led them into an office they'd been in before.

Ungaro looked up from a desk now littered with scrolls and books. Kara looked around but there were no tan or grey-black spells left in the space.

"It went well?" Ungaro asked.

"Yes," Santos said. "Kara?"

"Here's what I found." Kara wiped her palms on her skirt and glanced at Reo, who stood near the door. Even though she was relieved that her report wouldn't affect him, she was still nervous. Ungaro was a powerful man in charge of a powerful guild. She hadn't had a lot of good experiences with people in that kind of position.

"There were malicious spells in many of the public spaces," Kara said. "Many of the spells in this office were sent by Rorik, which I understand will not surprise you. The Hall of Records had the most spells but I removed only a few of them."

"Thank you," Ungaro said. "Can I ask just how malicious the spells were?"

"Some, very," Kara replied. "I can only reliably read the most dangerous spells." She paused. "These weren't the most threatening spells I've come across but they were sent to do damage."

"What kind of damage?" Ungaro asked.

"That's not clear," Santos said. "Kara's talent is unique, which is why you are so interested in her services. As she develops her abilities she may be able to tell what a spell is for, but today, it is beyond her. She has only been an Apprentice for a few weeks."

"Of course," Ungaro said. "And I am grateful for what you have done for my guild today." He turned to Jacopo. "Please see our guests to the pier."

THE TRIP BACK to Old Rillidi was quiet. Reo hopped onto the dock at home and reached out a hand to Kara.

"Thank you," he said as he helped her up. "For what you did today."

She nodded, not meeting his eyes, as Santos stepped onto the dock beside them.

"Yes," Santos said. "Thank you. Now, I think we all deserve the rest of the day off. Kara, I will see you in my study tomorrow morning. What do you think is left for lunch?" He headed off towards the garden and the door to the kitchen.

"Are you all right?" Reo asked. "I thought it important for you to see the contract. From your mother."

Kara sighed. "It's nothing I didn't already know," she replied. "But it made it more real, seeing a record of it. But I'm glad I did. You were right about that." She glanced up at him and smiled a sad smile. "But right now, I'm tired. I'll be at my cabin in case anyone needs me."

Reo nodded, and she turned, walked the length of the pier, and stepped down onto the rocky shore and the path that led to her cabin. Once there, she sat staring out at the bay until the sun went down and the light faded.

Chapter Two

THE EXIT WAS right . . . here. He reached out to where he thought the passageway would be—where it *should* be—but his hand found nothing but rough rock walls.

Where was it? Who had moved it? He shuffled forward, his hand trailing along the wall.

It was dark—he thought it must be night time, although it was usually dark in . . . here. Wherever here, was. He didn't know where he was, didn't know how he'd gotten here. Right now, he didn't even know who he was.

"Hello?" someone called from further down the hallway. A light from beyond a bend in the tunnel spilled onto the rock wall. "Are you there?"

"Here," he croaked, wondering if he'd really heard them. "I'm coming." He rounded the bend and the glare of a light almost blinded him. Had he found the exit? Was he finally heading outside?

"There you are," someone said from behind the light. "Did you find the way out?"

"Do I know you?" he asked, squinting past the light at a man with dark skin and long white hair that hung below his shoulders in braids. "Do you know me?" He didn't remember knowing *anyone*. But he'd known people at one time, hadn't he?

"Yes, we have met," the dark man said. "More than once, I'm

afraid. You are a Mage. And you've been looking for a way out for days."

"Days? Have I only been here for days?" He didn't remember being anywhere else, ever, so how was it possible he'd only been here for days? "A Mage? So, I can do magic?"

"Yes," the dark man replied. "You can do magic. Do you remember how? That's the way out. You'll need to create a spell in order to make a way out."

"I need the exit," he replied. "I've been looking for the way out. I know it's around here somewhere."

"You need to *make* an exit," the dark man said. "Through the rock, with magic. You will not be able to find one. Here," he held something out to him. "Have some water."

He eyed the waterskin that was being held out to him. What if it contained poison? But why would it? His companion seemed a reasonable man. He took the waterskin and drank deeply. He handed it back when he'd had enough.

"How do you know I will not find a way out?" he asked.

"I've looked," came the reply. "We've both looked. There is no way out."

"How can there be no way out? How did we get in here?"

"There was a way in," the dark man said. "At least, there was one from the outside. That's how I got in here. I came in through it, but once I was inside, I could not see any passageway that leads out."

"How is that possible?"

"Magic," the dark man replied. "It was a spell that you created."

"How do you know I created it?" If he was a Mage, why didn't he know that? Wouldn't he know if he really could do magic?

He waved his hand, and the man jumped out of the way. There was a loud crash from further down the hall. "Did I do that? I did that, didn't I?" He was excited now: he'd done magic. But what had the magic done? He hadn't tried to make it do anything specific, so what had it done?

"See," the dark man said. "You can do magic. And I know it's your magic because I can see it. I can see all of the magic around us and it's all the same colour. It's all your colour."

"I'll need some time to learn how to use my magic," he said. "Then I will do as you suggest and create a spell to make a way out."

He needed darkness for this, he could feel it. And maybe a nap. Then he would wake refreshed and ready to learn how to be a Mage.

AFTER THE TRIP to Warrior Guild, Kara redoubled her efforts to master her talent. It was slow, and there were still so many unknowns, but she was making progress. Even Santos agreed. Usually.

"I think you're too tired right now," Santos said. "We should start back in the morning."

"Just a few more spells," Kara replied, shoving her hair off her face in order to meet the Mage's eyes. "I should be able to do this when I'm tired, shouldn't I? Just like I should be able to ignore distractions?"

"Yes." Santos sighed. "But *I'm* tired. I need my supper and then I need to rest." He stood up and stretched. "I don't seem to have the stamina I had before I was cursed."

"Oh Gyda, I'm sorry." Kara peered at her mentor. How could she have been so inconsiderate? She spent energy on detecting the intent of spells but Santos had to spend energy in order to create them for her. They weren't completely certain that being cursed had affected his health, but his poor eating habits when he was mad would have. "Are you all right? Can I get you anything?"

"I would appreciate it if you could see what's for supper," Santos said. "I fear we've missed it again."

"Right away," Kara replied, heading for the door of the workroom. "I'll make you something if there's nothing left."

"Pilo?" she called as she entered the kitchen. "There you are. Is there any supper left for Santos?" Kara usually cooked and ate her supper in her cabin, joining the rest of them for breakfast and lunch, but it was late, so she wouldn't turn down a warm meal she didn't have to prepare but only if there was enough for Santos.

Pilo turned from the stove, where a pot was still simmering.

"There's plenty of stew," Pilo said. "Rabbit this time, thanks to Reo." She smiled and Kara took a moment to study the younger girl's face.

The scars were definitely fading, thanks to Santos' spell. And had the spell thinned out? She took a step towards Pilo.

"Can I take a look?" she asked. "I think it might be time for Santos to create another spell." She reached out a hand. Pilo flinched, briefly, before she closed her eyes and pressed her lips together.

When Kara's hand came close, the mage mist became even more transparent until it faded to nothing.

"Now I've done it," Kara said. She hadn't meant to remove the rest of the spell, but it had been very weak.

"Done what?" Santos asked as he entered the kitchen. "Something smells good. I hope there's enough left."

"I'll get bowls," Pilo said. "Kara, are you staying?"

"Yes," Santos replied. "I want to see you eat," he said to Kara. "You're looking a little thin." He pulled up a stool and sat down at the counter. "Now, what is it that you've done?"

Kara sat beside him while Pilo served them each a bowl of fragrant stew and thick slices of bread.

"Pilo's healing spell," Kara said. "It dissolved when I went to look at it. You'll need to redo it." She ate a spoonful of stew and sighed. Even without proper ingredients, Pilo had always been able to cook a decent stew, but now that she had spices and her pick of ingredients, they were exceptional.

"I'll create a new one," Santos replied. He spooned some stew into his mouth and chewed. "That will encourage a deeper, more complete healing." He continued to eat as he studied Pilo, who seemed uncomfortable at being the topic of conversation. "How do you feel, Pilo? Do your scars hurt?"

"They itch, a little," Pilo replied. "Just as you warned me. But they are so much better. And my fingers." She held out her hand and spread her fingers. The two that had been fused together with scar tissue were now separate. "I never thought I would have a normal hand. I don't even remember what it was like. Thank you."

"I'm happy to help," Santos said. "Your injuries should have been healed years ago." He held up his empty bowl. "But to thank me, more stew would not be unwelcome."

Pilo grinned and grabbed Santos' bowl. Kara tore off a piece of bread and started sopping up the leftover gravy.

She'd just popped the bread in her mouth when something made her turn around.

Reo stood by the door that led into the house, a serious look on his face.

"Santos, Kara," Reo said. "I'm sorry to interrupt your meal, but we have visitors. When you're finished eating, can you meet us in the front parlour?"

"I'll come now," Kara said. "Santos can join us when he's done."

"Thank you." Reo turned and left. Kara glanced at Santos, who shrugged as he dug into his stew, before she followed Reo out of the kitchen.

Reo paced beside her as they headed along the corridor that led to the parlour. A large room where comfortable couches and overstuffed chairs ringed an enormous fireplace, it was in the part of the estate that had never been damaged.

"Who is it?" Kara asked Reo. "Does Santos know them? Do I know them?"

"Yes," he replied. "And it's you they've come to see." He paused outside the door to the parlour and looked over at her. "And whatever your decision, I will support it—and you—in any way I can."

Nervous now, Kara entered the parlour. Two men stood near the fireplace.

"Javan Losi?" Kara asked. "Is that you?"

Javan bowed before heading toward her with a grin.

"Kara Fonti," he said, grabbing her hands. "You are still my most impressive theft: stolen from Mage Guild as they hunted you."

"I hope it didn't cause you any trouble," she replied. She was genuinely happy to see the Seyoyan and would always be grateful to him. He had been responsible for saving her and Reo's lives; first by plucking them out of the sea and then by keeping them safe from Mage Guild. "And who is your companion—" The smile slid off her face. "Sif Shadae." Her heart sank. "I didn't know you and Javan were friends." She'd met him when she'd first arrived in Rillidi; he'd been with Chal on the ferry.

"You remember me," Sif said. He smiled a sad smile. "Javan and I were not well acquainted before current events." He gestured to a couch. "Please, sit down."

Kara sat down, knowing that she would not like this conversation. "Something's happened to Chal."

"We think so," Sif replied. "Although we're not sure what. He was sent to investigate something, and he has not been seen nor heard from since."

"It was magic, wasn't it? That's why Chal was needed, because there was magic."

"Yes," Javan agreed. "There are not so many of us who can see spells. Chal was sent because he has stronger skills than I do. And now that he has disappeared, I've been charged with discovering what happened to him." He paused. "But I do not want to blindly repeat his actions and suffer the same fate."

"Sending someone with a weaker gift after him seemed like a foolish thing to do," Sif said. "Javan and I agreed that we need someone with more powerful abilities."

"You want me to go," Kara said. "Yes." She didn't even have to think about it. Chal was her friend. They'd met under difficult circumstances but he'd only ever been kind to her during the months she'd spent with him and Reo. She would help him.

"It will be dangerous," Reo said.

"I don't care." She turned to him. "You'll come with me." That's what he'd meant, when he'd said he would support her and her decision.

"Of course," Reo replied.

"Then it's settled," Kara said. "When do we leave?"

"I see my Apprentice is making plans without me," Santos said from the doorway. "Again."

"Santos." Kara stood and faced him. "Of course, we need your advice."

Santos walked toward her. He gripped her hands. "But not my permission?" He shrugged. "You must do what you need to do. That's part of what makes you exceptional." He let go of her hands and sat in a chair. "Now, I think we should hear the details of what's happened so we can determine what to do next."

"It was me," Javan said. "I saw it first." He turned to Kara. "How much do you know about Seyoya?"

"Quite a lot, thanks to Chal," Kara replied. "It's made up of dozens of islands, covering a very large area. Each island has a local Small Council who then form a Large Council that makes decisions on trade and settles disputes over fishing rights, among other things."

"Yes," Javan said. "But not every island is inhabited." He

paused. "One day I sailed past one of those uninhabited islands. And it was covered in mage mist. It took me a moment to realize what I was seeing; the mist was such a pale blue that it seemed little more than a fog, or a reflection of the sky or water. I reported it to the Large Council and then didn't give it any further thought."

"The Large Council decided to have Chal investigate," Sif said. "That's when he was called home. Reo had been released from Warrior Guild so Chal was available."

"He came to say goodbye," Kara said. "Almost a month ago."

"Yes. He spent some time at home before meeting with the Large Council," Sif said. "I was on the ship that dropped him off on the island. He has not been seen since."

"How long has he been missing?" Reo asked.

"Just over a week," Sif replied. "We waited two days for a signal from him; then we landed on the island. We didn't dare go very far, considering that none of us could see what we were stepping into."

"This island is on my regular trade route," Javan said. "I was sailing past when Sif's ship flagged us down. The two of us went to the Large Council to report Chal's disappearance while the other ship stayed at the island in case he returned to where he landed."

"The council gave us permission to act as we see fit," Sif said. He looked over at Javan. "We both agreed that you, Kara, are the best hope of finding Chal."

"What provisions did Chal have with him?" Reo asked, and Kara stared at him, her worry increasing.

What if Chal was already out of water and food? What if they were already too late to find and help him? Too late to save him?

"We need to leave tomorrow at first light," Kara said.

"Chal had a month's supply of food," Sif replied. "And records show that the island has many water sources—streams and springs—that he would have access to."

"So, he has maybe two weeks of food left," Reo said. "Kara is right; we need to leave as soon as possible. Santos," Reo turned to the Mage, "what are your thoughts?"

"You and Kara must go," Santos said. "Kara can take care of any magic or Mages you may encounter. I need to stay and make sure that Old Rillidi is protected."

"You think Mage Guild might be responsible for this?" Kara asked.

"We can't rule it out," Santos replied. "It doesn't sound like a tactic Rorik would come up with, but I don't know Arabella Fonti well enough to say that she couldn't have planned this."

"I wouldn't put anything past my mother," Kara said. Her mother wanted her dead—she was certain Arabella would be willing to hurt her friends in order to cause her grief. Or lure her and Santos away from Old Rillidi and then attack it and destroy everything her daughter cared about.

IT WAS SUNNY—*a good start to the day*, Kara thought as she packed a few things into a bag. In her kitchen, she tucked the few perishables that she had into a basket. She'd leave these in the kitchen of the estate house. No doubt Pilo could find a use for them. Both she and Pilo had gone hungry enough times that letting food spoil was unthinkable.

She paused at the open door, looking over her cosy cabin one last time before pulling the door shut. It would be here when she returned; Santos would see to that.

The kitchen was busy. Sidra, Mole, Osten, and Giona were chattering around mouthfuls of porridge. Vook hovered over the stove, stirring a pot. The two Seyoyans stood in a corner, looking bemused.

"Are you sure you can spare this, Pilo?" Reo, carrying three loaves of bread, stepped out of the storeroom, followed by Pilo.

"Yes," Pilo said. "This bunch will just have to do without until I can make more. And there's a basket of apples and some carrots. How long will you be gone?"

"A few weeks I think," Reo said. "Javan said that although the ship is fully stocked, fresh bread as well as apples and carrots will be appreciated by the crew. Sorry to be depleting your stores."

"I'm adding to them," Kara said. She put her basket on the counter. "Besides, Pilo can always buy bread if she needs to."

"I hate doing that," Pilo said. "But I can. And I know it helps the town."

"Should we be buying bread?" Reo asked.

"It won't be ready until later today," Kara replied. "And we want to leave as soon as possible, don't we?"

"Yes," Sif said. "The earlier the better. Mage Guild tends to spend less time inspecting ships that leave early. We think it might be because a specific Mage is on duty at that time of day, but we prefer to take advantage of it, whatever the reason."

"I forgot about their inspections," Kara said. "Hey!" She caught Osten's arm as he was about to dash past her. "I'm leaving for a few weeks, so you be good." Osten stared at her before he nodded and raced out the kitchen door.

"I'll watch him, Kara." Giona paused beside her. "Gyda's luck to you."

"Thank you," she replied, but Giona had already left the kitchen.

"Here." Vook set a bowl of porridge down in front of her and handed her a spoon. "Travel safe and come back soon."

"That's the idea," she agreed. She let Reo and Pilo handle the rest of the provisioning while she ate.

Sif and Javan took the bags from Pilo. "We'll be at the pier," Javan said. He led Sif through the door to the back garden.

Kara peered out the window. A ship was moored in the bay, midway between the manor house and Warrior Guild Island.

"Do you see any signs that Mage Guild has noticed it?" Reo asked, coming to stand beside her.

"I don't see any mage mist," Kara replied. She ate one last spoonful of porridge. "Not at the moment, anyway."

KARA WATCHED FOR mage mist from the prow of the small boat. The bay was rough and waves slapped against the boat, sending salty spray into the air as the Seyoyans rowed them towards the ship. But by the time she stepped onto the deck of the ship she'd seen no sign of mage mist: no sign that Mage Guild was suspicious of the ship. Because Warrior Guild hired Seyoyans, they did have legitimate business with them that even Mage Guild couldn't challenge, so perhaps they hadn't bothered to investigate.

She joined Javan, who stood on deck beside an older Seyoyan man whose wide-brimmed hat shaded his eyes.

"Kara Fonti," Javan said. "This is Captain Bogan Arends, captain of the *Mizar*. He'll be taking us to Seyoya."

"Captain," Kara said. "I believe Reo and I have been on your ship before." She'd been half-drowned when she'd boarded it the last time, but she thought she recognized the carved railings.

"You have." The captain took her hand and bowed over it, his white braids sweeping almost to the deck. When he straightened, she saw what looked like slivers of shells twisted into his braids. "It is again my pleasure to transport you and Reo Medina." He nodded to Reo, who had just joined them. "Unfortunately, you both must hide below decks until we are well away from Rillidi."

"This way," Javan said. "At the moment, I fear I cannot even offer accommodations equal to what you had your last time aboard. Ever since we helped you escape from Mage Guild Island, Seyoyan ships have often been searched when we leave Rillidi. We have a small secret compartment that will hide you in case we are boarded for inspection." He showed the way to narrow stairs that led below. Kara followed him, Reo close behind her.

Once down the stairs, Javan crossed a hold filled with barrels and crates. The smell of old fish scented the air.

"Do you expect to be boarded?" Kara asked.

"Merchant Guild does not inspect every ship leaving these waters," Javan said. "But it's frequent enough that we must be prepared."

"And Mage Guild?" Reo asked. "Do they inspect?"

"Often," Javan agreed. "But they do it magically." He stopped in front of a blank wall. "You must hide yourselves from that." He reached up and activated a latch of some kind, and a portion of the wall lifted out and up. "I hope it's not too uncomfortable for you," he said, stepping back from the wall.

Kara peered inside. Two hammocks were strung up side by side with very little space between them. The ceiling in the windowless room was far too low to allow Kara to stand, and the light that streamed in from the opening she stood in front of was the only illumination. But the air smelled of the sea, so she didn't think it was a tightly sealed room.

"The hammocks are quite comfortable," Javan said. "But they are more to make sure that nothing—even in rough weather—hits the walls and makes a sound that can be heard by inspectors."

"We're not the first people you've transported this way?" Reo asked.

"You know how Seyoyans like to steal," Javas said with a grin. "Anything and everything. Now, please get in. Captain Arends will not get under way until I tell him you're stowed away."

Kara crawled to one of the hammocks. It took her a few tries, but eventually, she hauled herself into the one on the left. Reo bumped into her a few times as he climbed into the other one.

"I'll come fetch you as soon as it's safe," Javan said. The light disappeared as he closed the wall opening, leaving Kara and Reo in pitch dark.

Kara tried to relax. She closed her eyes then opened them. She needed to be awake and aware in case Mages sent spells to inspect the ship.

Faint shouts drifted to her from the deck above, and after a few moments, she felt the ship move. Her hammock started to swing as the ship dipped and rose as it crossed waves. The wood creaked, and she heard waves crashing against the hull.

"Hold on," Reo whispered.

She reached out and found his hand, and he gripped hers, pulling the hammocks closer. Together, they steadied a little, and Kara took a deep breath. Her stomach felt a little unsettled, but now that the side to side motion had decreased, she could better deal with the rise and fall of the ship as it plowed through waves.

"Close your eyes if you feel nauseated," Reo said.

"I can't," she replied. "I need to watch for mage mist."

Reo didn't answer, but simply squeezed her hand. Kara tried not to read too much into that simple gesture but she did squeeze back.

The ship rolled to one side, and Kara's hammock—with her in it—swung, wedging her against Reo.

"We must be rounding past Rillidi Port," Reo whispered in her ear. "Merchant Guild Island is next, so we'll know soon if they're going to stop us and inspect the ship."

The ship slowed but didn't stop. It rolled onto its other side, and now Kara was slightly under Reo. She suppressed a giggle, but he must have felt it anyway, because he laughed.

She was about to say something in response when she noticed a light seeping in through the hull near her head. She gripped Reo's hand.

"Mage mist," she whispered into his ear.

So pale a yellow that it almost looked white, tendrils of mage mist oozed between the wooden planks. Without a thought, she pulled Reo closer; he reached an arm around her, pulling her head onto his shoulder.

Should she destroy the spell or would the Mage who'd sent it know their spell was gone and sound the alarm? Better to have it ignore them. She concentrated on keeping the spell away from them, and the mist twisted and flowed past them.

Kara lifted her head off Reo's chest and watched as the thick rope of mage mist stretched and thinned as it travelled away from them, through the wall and into the hold.

With a sigh, she dropped her head back onto Reo.

"It's gone," she said.

They didn't move for the half hour they waited in silence. Kara was aware of Reo's steady heartbeat under her head and his arm around her shoulder, keeping her pressed against him.

Even when she was sure the threat was over, she didn't move—didn't want to move—away from his warmth.

A grating sound made her lift her head, and she rolled back into her own hammock just as the light from the opening hit her.

"We are clear of both Merchant and Mage Guilds," Javan said. "Did any spells come this way?"

"Yes," Kara replied. "I kept it away from us." She tried to get out of the hammock and would have fallen if Reo hadn't grabbed her. He helped her onto the floor, and she backed out of the small compartment.

She stood up, brushing dust from her trousers, ignoring the coolness of the air after being pressed against Reo's warmth.

"Can we go on deck?" Kara asked. "I would like some fresh air."

"Yes, of course. Tregella and Rillidi are behind us, and there is nothing but sea ahead." Javan closed the door to the compartment. "Come, this way. I will show you to your cabins, and then we can go on deck."

Kara was aware of Reo's silence as they both followed Javan through the ship. They exited the hold and walked along a hallway and then up a short set of stairs.

"This is your cabin, Kara." Javan opened a door to a cabin not much larger than the compartment they'd hidden in, although she was able to stand up in it. A narrow bunk was suspended from ropes and a small wash basin was attached to one wall. Her bag sat on the bunk. A similar cabin across the hall was for Reo.

The tour included the galley, where the food was prepared and served, along with the dining area, and the head, before Javan took them on deck.

Kara breathed in the sea air and closed her eyes, enjoying the wind in her hair.

"You can just make out Rillidi if you look behind us," Reo said.

Kara turned to see a dark splotch along the horizon: Mage Guild Island. She shaded her eyes as she watched the land recede.

Her plan—her mother's plan—had been for her to board a ship and find a home somewhere else. She could still do it, if she wanted to. She had people she cared about like family—and a brother—but they would be fine without her. In fact, they might be *safer* without her, if her mother and Rorik were told that she was truly gone. She turned to find Reo watching her.

"Have you been on a ship before?" she asked. "Sailing away somewhere, not just being rescued."

"Yes. That's how I met Chal." He sighed and looked back towards Rillidi. "It was about four years ago. Warrior Guild gave me time and resources to see if I could find and convince a Seyoyan to come and work with me."

"I thought Seyoyans hired Warriors?"

Reo grinned and she smiled in response. She hadn't seen him look so carefree in a long time.

"That's what Warrior Guild tells everyone," he said. "So other guilds don't try to hire them."

Kara shook her head. "Chal kept a lot of secrets from me. But he was always kind."

"Even when I wasn't," Reo said and sighed. "He helped you in the Old Rillidi market when I would have left you to fend for yourself." He turned and looked at her. "Sometimes I think it would have been for the best if I had made him walk away from you. You would have been a few items of clothing poorer, but safer. Your mother would never have known that you were alive."

"She would have found me eventually," Kara said. "Besides, good things happened because Chal helped me; because you found me and we struck our bargain." She shrugged. "My brother Osten was saved from a horrible life. Valerio Valendi is dead. My mother is Mage Guild Secundus, but I don't believe she's as evil— as destructive—as he was. And don't forget that Santos has regained his sanity and has vowed to protect everyone on Old Rillidi from all of the guilds, especially Mage Guild." *And I met you*, she thought.

"I suppose," he said. "I have a lot to regret—"

"Don't," Kara said. "We've had this argument before. I bear some of the responsibility for what happened. But no matter how difficult things were, we made it through them—together—and good things happened because of that." She took a deep breath and met his eyes. "Life on Old Rillidi is better because of that. *We* are better because of that. We're also better when we work together." Unable to hold his gaze any longer, she turned and fled to the safety of her cabin.

She lay on her bunk and closed her eyes, determined not to cry—again—but a few tears tracked down her cheek.

Why couldn't Reo see the good that had happened—the good that they had helped make happen? Instead, he continued to concentrate on mistakes he'd made, as though he was the only person who had ever made an error in judgement. As though his actions were the only reasons for the danger they'd found themselves in. She'd forgiven her own mistakes weeks ago, just as she'd forgiven him his. So why couldn't he forgive himself?

Maybe she should stay in Seyoya, just for a while. She'd miss Santos and Osten and Pilo and the rest of them. She'd miss her magical little cabin, too. But she wouldn't have to know that Reo was within reach but that he was unreachable by her.

Chapter Three

THE EXIT WAS right . . . here. He reached out to where he thought the passageway would be—where it *should* be—but his hand found nothing but rough rock walls.

A light glowed up ahead. Was the way out there?

"Hello?" he called. "Is anyone here?" Wherever *here* was. He shuffled towards the light, yawning. Had he just woken up? What time of day was it?

A man lay on the dirt of the cave floor, squinting up at him.

"Hello," he said to him. The man's skin was dark, and he had white hair that gleamed in the light.

He looked more closely at the light. It wasn't a flame—it was a globe of light.

"Is that light magic?" he asked the dark man.

"Yes." The man's voice was resigned as he sat up and leaned against the cave wall. "You made it for me a few days ago."

"I did? I can do magic?" He stared at his arm; his skin was pale while his companion's was dark. "Did I make you dark? Or did I make me light?"

His companion laughed. "No, we are from different parts of the world. I am Seyoyan and you are Tregellan."

"Tregellan." His mouth seemed to find the word familiar, although he wasn't exactly sure what it meant. "I'm a Mage." That sounded right too although he couldn't remember how to do magic.

"Yes, you are a Mage," his companion said. "If you can remember how to create spells, then you can create an exit and allow us to escape."

"Escape," he repeated. "Yes, I would like to escape. Can you teach me how to create spells? I would like to escape."

"I don't know how, but if you figure out or remember the first step, tell me. That way I can explain it to you after the next time you've slept."

"I will," he said. "I should try to make another light, since you say I can make them. I need some tools, don't I?" He must have left his tools . . . back where he'd been? "I shall look for them."

"Don't go to sleep," his companion said. "Not until you tell me the first step in doing magic."

"Never fear," he called over his shoulder. He had no plans to sleep. He'd just woken up, hadn't he? He stifled a yawn as he headed back into the darkness. He was feeling tired though. He'd just find his tools, figure out the first step to creating magic spells, and then let the man know. Then he'd have a quick nap.

He took a few more steps and yawned again. A nap wasn't really sleep, was it? He could have just a quick nap and then find his tools. He lay down on the dirt floor, in the dark, and closed his eyes. Just a very quick nap.

Kara stayed in her cabin the next day. It wasn't to avoid seeing Reo, although that was a consequence she was grateful for. No, she stayed in her cabin because she wasn't well enough to leave it.

Once they reached the open seas, her gut had started to churn. She'd lain in her bunk, rolling and tossing with the waves, trying to keep down what little was in her stomach.

Javan visited her a few times to see how she was faring and to make sure she was drinking enough water. He hadn't had good news about the weather, though, so she'd worried that her misery would never end.

But then it did, and she woke up ravenous.

She quickly dressed in a shirt and trousers that seemed a little looser, and then headed up the half flight of stairs to the galley. She was on her third bowl of porridge before she felt even a little sated.

She finished eating, pushed her bowl away, and looked up to see Sif smiling at her from the doorway.

"I take it you're feeling better?" he asked.

"Much, thank you." Kara reached for the water jug and poured herself a mug. "Does everyone who sails feel as wretched as I did?"

"No, some have it worse." Sif sat down across from her, placing two steaming mugs on the table. "And the rare person feels nothing. You are about average, I'd guess." He pushed one of the mugs towards her. "And in luck, since I just made tea."

"Thank you." Kara picked up the mug and took a sip. "Are we far from the island Chal was sent to?" Now that she felt better it was time to plan on how to would find her friend.

"Based on the weather, another day or so, according to Javan," Sif said. "Ah, Reo, there you are. Come, now that Kara is up and about, we need to discuss the search for Chal."

Kara glanced up as Reo sat down beside Sif.

"Is the island small enough that we can sail around it?" Kara asked. "I'd like to determine the best place to land."

"Chal was set ashore at the best place to land," Sif replied.

"She means based on the amount of mage mist," Reo said. "Don't you, Kara?"

"Yes." She ignored a small surge of anger. Reo hadn't bothered to check on her when she was ill, so why did he now feel that he could speak for her? "And by sailing around the island I hope to be able to tell whether we are dealing with a single Mage or if there is more than one to worry about."

"I'll have to defer to Javan," Sif replied. "And Captain Arends. I'm not sure it will be possible to take the ship all the way around the island. At least not close enough to it for you see what you need to."

"If not, we'll take a dory," Reo said. "If Kara says she needs to go around the island, then that's what we'll do."

"I'll let Javan know," Sif said and stood up.

Kara sipped her tea, almost hoping that Reo would follow Sif out of the galley. When he didn't, she debated whether she would leave first.

"I'm glad you're feeling better," Reo said. "I would have visited but I wasn't sure . . ." he trailed off.

"Javan took good care of me," Kara said stiffly. She took

another sip of her now cool tea.

"Good," Reo said. She thought he would leave now but instead he leaned over the table to her.

"I've . . ." he paused. "I've had time to think about what you said in our last conversation. You're right, things are better because of what happened. And Tregella is safer with your mother as Secundus rather than Valendi. But I can't forgive myself for what I put you through, and I can't see how I can make amends." Abruptly, he stood up and walked away.

Kara stared at his retreating back. Why did he never ask her what she wanted? If he felt the need to make amends for his past decisions, all he had to do was ask. She could think of plenty of ways he could repay the debt he felt he owed her. The first on the list would be to agree to start over and not have the same argument every time they spoke.

She slumped on the bench, her head in her hands. Chal had told her to give Reo time, that the former Assassin was acting the way he was because he cared so *much* about her, not that he cared so little.

Kara wanted to believe that but she was losing patience—and hope. She'd thought that on this trip they would, of course, save Chal, but she'd also hoped—assumed, actually—that she and Reo would become real friends. She'd also had faith that their friendship would naturally lead to more. But Reo didn't seem to want what she wanted.

She sighed. And what did she want from Reo? She knew she wanted this awkwardness between them to disappear, but what did she want to replace it?

His friendship wouldn't be enough for her. She sighed. She'd never completely and honestly admitted that to herself before; never admitted that she'd always had some vague idea that they would just somehow end up as a couple. Even Chal's advice had implied that, so she had to admit that yes, she wanted Reo's love. Did that mean she loved him? Was that why it hurt so much when he couldn't—or wouldn't—get past what he thought were his unforgivable actions?

They would reach the island soon. At that point, finding Chal would be the only important goal. She'd expected to be able to trust Reo—to know that they were a team—when they landed there. Now she was wondering what she had to do to make that a reality.

And why should she give Reo time to figure things out when she knew what she wanted?

She grinned; she really must be feeling better. She wasn't going to let Reo set the terms of their relationship any more. She was tired of waiting; now she would act.

Feeling happier than she had since she'd boarded the ship, Kara took her empty dishes to the wash tub before heading up on deck.

Reo was at the rail, staring out at sea. She didn't join him. Instead, she walked a few steps past him before she too took up position at the rail and stared out at the horizon.

She was no longer going to avoid him; nor would she allow him to avoid her. They were on a small ship—there were very few places for him to hide.

SHE TRIED TO be casual about it, but she was certain Reo knew that she was following him around, although he didn't say anything to her.

When he went to one side of the ship, she strolled that way a few moments later. When he had his lunch in the galley, she happened to be hungry at the exact same time. When he needed a warm cup of tea, so did she.

By the time dinner was ready, she'd trailed him from one end of the ship to the other more than a few times. And yet he didn't confront her about it.

When he rose after eating, she decided to leave him alone for the night. They were on a ship—she'd find him in the morning.

AFTER BREAKFAST, KARA stepped out onto the deck, but when she saw Reo, she turned around and descended to the lower level of the ship and made her way to her cabin.

Once there, she sat on the bed, her feet hanging off the edge, swinging as the ship rode up and down over the waves.

She'd thought following Reo around—making him see her—was the right thing to do, but now, she just felt sad.

She sighed. She wanted his love because she loved him. But that was not something she could make him feel for her: just as she couldn't make her mother love her. Just as she couldn't make herself stop loving him.

And he was right, in a way. She probably *shouldn't* love him—he'd forced her into a bargain that she hadn't wanted and then had bedded her for reasons that had nothing to do with his feelings for her and everything to with his goals. And in the process, he'd taken away her independence.

But she'd taken it back, and he didn't seem to understand that. She'd risked his wrath—the fury of an Assassin—in order to assert her independence. Then he'd made a mistake—out of anger—and taken her to see her mother. But from that point on he'd done everything he could, including risking his life, to keep her safe.

And yesterday she had childishly followed him around the ship trying to force him to see what they could have together, and in the process, took away some of his independence. He deserved so much better from her.

She sighed again. Chal had said to give him time, but would she be able to stand waiting for a day that might never come? She got off the bed, a decision made, and headed out into the narrow hall.

She passed a couple of doors before she stopped and knocked on one. The door swung open, and Sif stood in the doorway, looking at her expectantly.

"Kara, what can I do for you?"

"Chal once told me that I would be in demand as a teacher in Seyoya," she said before she could lose her nerve. "He said Seyoyans would pay for my knowledge of the Guilds. After we rescue Chal, I would like to go to Seyoya and see if that is true. Can I count on your help?"

"Of course," Sif said. "I'd be honoured. Is Reo—"

"This is about me," Kara said. "My life and my decision." She paused, thinking that perhaps she'd been a little too harsh. "I'm not saying I'll stay in Seyoya forever, but a year, maybe six months away seems like an adventure, don't you think?"

"Of course." Sif smiled. "I understand completely. I went to Tregella because adventure also calls to me. And to Chal, I might add. You can count on both of us."

"Thank you," Kara said. She turned away, feeling lighter than she had in a while. She'd send a message with Reo to tell Santos and the rest that she would return within a year. That should give her enough time to . . . do whatever she wanted. Be her own woman and take charge of her life.

With a smile, she headed up on deck. She didn't avoid Reo but neither did she seek him out. She simply enjoyed the sun on her face and the wind in her hair as the ship sailed towards Seyoya.

THE EXIT WAS right . . . here. He reached out to where he thought the passageway would be—where it *should* be—but his hand found nothing but rough rock walls.

He scratched his head, wondering why he was so sure there would be a way out. Did that mean he was inside somewhere? But inside where?

"There you are," someone said from behind him.

He turned to see a dark-skinned man holding a light in one hand.

"Do I know you?" he asked. The man seemed familiar, but he didn't know how that was possible.

"Yes," the dark man replied. "I'm to give you a message. You need to collect energy. I'm not sure how, but you need to do that."

"Am I? Who told you to give me this message?"

"You did," the dark man replied. "It's the first step to creating a spell. To doing magic."

"I told you?" He didn't remember telling him anything. "And I know how to create spells?"

"You do, but you've forgotten," the man said. "You forget every time you sleep." The dark man shrugged his shoulders, making the light bob slightly.

"You look very tired," he said to the dark man. "And sad. Is it because I forget? Shouldn't I be sad about that too? Ohh, I forget to be sad." He probed his mind for anything he could remember. "The exit. I need to use magic to make a way for us to get out."

"That's right," the dark man said. "So if you can figure out the next step and tell me, I can tell you both steps the next time you wake up."

"That sounds like a very good idea," he said. "I'll need a quiet place to concentrate."

"I'll just be around the bend," the dark man said. "Don't go to sleep until you know the next step." He took the light and disappeared around a corner.

Light still spilled out, bathing the wall. He sat down and tried to collect energy. He wasn't sure what that meant, and he didn't feel anything. Had he collected energy? He was tired so he assumed he had.

"I did it," he called. "I've collected energy." Now what to do next? He yawned. Now he was certain that he had done something—why else was he so exhausted? Perhaps he'd better have a nap. He lay down with his head resting on his arm. He was drifting off to sleep when he remembered that the dark man had told him not to go to sleep.

Now that she'd made a decision, Kara felt much better. She was pretty sure Reo sensed a change in her attitude, and she would have been happy to discuss it with him—she would have to eventually because he was going to explain her actions to Santos and Osten and Pilo. But as usual, he didn't talk to her about it, just as he didn't talk to her about anything other than the guilt he felt over taking her to see her mother.

Javan came by to tell her that the island where Chal was lost would be in view in an hour, so she headed to the prow of the ship to wait for her first glimpse of it.

"Pale blue," Kara said. The island was smaller than she'd expected, and hillier. Even from this distance she could see a rocky cliff. Palm trees seemed to cover most of the land and blue mage mist swirled around them. "That's the only colour I see so far."

"That's what I remember," Javan said. "But your ability to see mage mist is better than mine."

"When do we need to launch the dory?" Kara asked. Captain Arends had determined that it was too dangerous to take the *Mizar* around the island close enough for her to get a good look at the shoreline.

"After we reach the small harbour," Javan said. "The ship can safely drop anchor there. That's where Chal went ashore."

"I still want to go all the way around the island before we set foot on it," Kara said. She turned to her other side. "Reo? Is that all right with you?"

"Yes," he agreed. He peered skyward. "We may even want to come back on board after. There might be enough mage mist for you to see by, but for the rest of us, it will be dark." He met her eyes. "But it will be your decision."

"That's reasonable," Kara replied. She sighed inwardly. Reo

was always reasonable—too reasonable—that was one of the issues she had with him. He didn't complain or confront her about anything. She blew out a breath and stared towards the island. Where was the man who wasn't afraid to make decisions? Who had things he wanted in life and then did his best to get them? Even a bad decision—like taking her to see her mother—was better than no decision, wasn't it?

"YOU HAVE THREE hours of daylight," Captain Arends said as Kara stepped over the gunwale.

Gripping the rope ladder, she met his steady gaze. "I hope we're back by then. Once I've seen the whole island, Reo and I will decide what to do next. And when." She stepped down the ladder into the dory. Gani, one the men assigned to row, helped her climb over the seats to the bow. Emek, the other rower, sat down on the seat in front of her. Reo followed her down and sat at the stern. Reo—with his experience steering Assassin boats—would pilot them while Kara looked for both physical and magical dangers.

It took a few strokes for the boat to get close enough to the island to see where Chal had landed. The small beach was clear of mage mist although it clung to some of the trees that lined it. Kara assumed it was Chal's boat that was pulled up onto the sand, up above the waves. He'd turned it over, so he must have planned to be away from it for a few days.

"How much food and water did Chal have with him?" Kara asked. She knew it had been discussed, but she hadn't wanted to know—hadn't wanted to treat this as anything but a rescue mission. But now that they were here, it seemed like critical information.

"He had food for around a month," Reo said. "And Javan said this island has plenty of springs, so water shouldn't be a problem." He pointed towards a sheer cliff face just past the beach. "There's a stream there." A trickle of water spilled off the cliff and into the sea below.

Once the boat was within twenty feet of the beach, they veered right, passing close to where the water splashed into the sea. The cliff had only a few patches of mage mist on it but the palm trees and bushes at the top were almost obscured by it.

The rowers kept them heading to the right. Waves lapped at

the sides of the boat, and the sea swirled and eddied closer to the island. Kara gripped the gunwales as the sea, combined with the choppy movement of rowing, threatened to slide her off her seat.

The cliff sloped downward until it was less than five feet above the sea. Chunks of the island had slid down, and the water close to shore was dotted with jagged rocks and lumps of earth. Mage mist was thick along the raw shoreline, and Kara wondered if magic had caused the landslide.

There was only a single colour of mage mist: pale blue. But Kara couldn't understand why a Mage would bother ruining this shoreline. What had the Mage been trying to do?

They saw more of the same for the next hour: land that had slid into the sea, making safe landing for any boat impossible. Most of the damage looked new: the wounds to the earth were fresh and any palm trees she saw still had green fronds.

Kara stared at another raw section of land that looked like it had had recently slid into the sea, and her heart sank.

"I know what it is," she said. She turned to face Reo. "I know what happened here." She looked back at the tree—or at least what once had been a tree. Its fronds were still green, so it had been changed recently but the trunk looked like it was made of glass. And although she'd never seen a tree changed like that before, it was still horribly familiar.

"There's a mad mage here," she said.

"Are you sure?" Reo asked.

"Not completely, no," Kara said, hoping she wasn't right. It would be so much better for Chal if she was wrong. "But see that tree? It has the look of what Santos did when he was mad."

"All right," Reo said, and she heard his sigh above the sounds of the waves. "Let me know where the worst of it is, so we can stay well clear."

It took them another hour to round the island and return to the *Mizar*. Kara saw two more trees that had been transformed as well as a rock slope that looked like it had been melted. How could there be another Mage who was mad? Had he become unstable naturally or had he been cursed, like Santos?

And with a mad mage on this island, did they dare hope that Chal was alive after all this time? And if he was alive, would a mad mage have somehow changed him?

Chapter Four

THE EXIT WAS right . . . here. He reached out to where he thought the passageway would be—where it *should* be—but his hand found nothing but rough rock walls.

"What do you remember?" someone asked from nearby.

"Who's there? Do I know you?" It was dark. It was always dark—wasn't it?

"It's me," the voice replied. "We've met many times."

"Why is it dark?" The man—it was a man—sounded very weary. Perhaps he wasn't able to sleep the way he was. Although he didn't feel exactly refreshed.

"The light went out," the man said. "You'll need to create another one. First, you need to collect the energy. Then you need to concentrate."

"I do? How do I do any of that?"

"Have some water," the man said. "And some journey bread. It's the last of it."

Something was thrust into his arms—a waterskin and a piece of hard bread. He took a sip of water. "That's much better, thank you." He gnawed on the bread, thinking about what the man had said. Collect energy. He raised his hand—he couldn't see it in the dark, but he could feel energy flowing into him.

"That's right," the man said. "Collect the energy. Then concentrate on making a passage that will lead us outside."

"Concentrate," he mumbled to himself. There was a flash, and he felt the energy rush out of him. A small globe hung overhead. "I did it!" he crowed. "I made a light!"

"Now try to make a way out," the man said. He was dark, his friend: he looked at his own hand, which was light-skinned.

"The exit?" He'd been looking for the exit, hadn't he? "It should be right here, shouldn't it?"

"You have to make it. With magic."

"I see." He yawned. Making the light had sapped all of his energy. Making a way out would be exhausting. Perhaps he should rest up a little.

"No, don't go to sleep," his companion said. "You can't go to sleep."

"But I'm tired." He'd just lie down for a moment. The man kept trying to keep him awake, but he was just so tired. His eyes drooped closed, and despite the hand that was shaking his shoulder, he slept.

Kara paced the length of the railing, every so often staring out at the mage mist that covered the island. She could deal with the spells—she had enough practice with that—but another mad mage? Santos had been sane part of the time—what if this Mage was mad all the time? And what happened to Chal?

"Captain asked if we can wait until morning," Reo said as he caught up to her. "When he'll be more than happy to lend us some men. But not until then."

"No." She stopped and turned to face Reo. "I don't need daylight. Set me down tonight, and I'll clear a path." She turned to look at the island. "You can come in the morning with the extra men."

When she heard Reo sigh, she relaxed. He wasn't going to argue with her.

"I'll come with you," Reo said. "And the men can follow tomorrow." He stood at her side, facing the island. "You think Chal is in more danger than we thought."

"I think we're all in more danger than we thought," she replied. "I'll get my cloak and some rations. I'll meet you at the dory."

The sun was going down in a blaze of yellow and orange and red by the time the dory was lowered back into the sea.

Kara stepped down into the boat, Reo's hand steadying her as she took a seat. Gani and Emek shifted the oars and started rowing them toward the island. The small beach where Chal's boat had been hauled ashore steadily got closer.

"Oars in," Emek said when they were a dozen yards away from the beach. He and Gani drew their oars into the boat, and then Gani jumped into the surf. He pulled the dory towards the beach, dragging them forward until Kara heard sand scuffing the bottom of the boat.

"Let's go," Reo said. With his boots slung over his shoulder, he headed to the prow and jumped into waist-deep water. With her own boots held against her chest, Kara awkwardly climbed over the gunwale and dropped into the surf.

Reo caught her shoulders and kept her upright until her feet found the sandy bottom.

"We'll be back in the morning," Gani said before he climbed back into the dory.

"I'll mark a path where Kara has cleared away the magic and it's safe to walk," Reo called over his shoulder.

As Kara waded to shore, the waves tugged at her legs, threatening to pull her off her feet. Once she reached land, she paused to look around.

Mage mist clung to some of the trees that surrounded the beach, but the sand itself was clear. She walked up to the nearest patch of mist and reached a hand toward it. She didn't feel anything from it: there was no sense of hate or ill intent. It didn't even seem focused.

Reo joined her.

"Wait until I clear away the mage mist," she said. "It's just in the trees, so the beach is safe."

All of the mage mist close to the beach had to be removed. Sailors might enter the trees to look for wood for a fire or dig a privy: she didn't want them to run into any magic. Just because she didn't feel any ill intent from this mage mist didn't mean it couldn't do harm.

Santos still didn't know if he was responsible for the burn out on Old Rillidi, and if he was, he hadn't meant to hurt anyone. But the fire had still caused terrible harm to property and people. Pilo was proof of that.

She sat down and brushed wet sand from her feet and slipped them into her boots. Beside her, Reo did the same. He held out his hand. She took it, and he pulled her up.

She walked along the trees that lined the beach, waving her arms, willing the magic to disappear. She stepped into the trees removing more mist. It dissolved readily enough—any underlying spells really were unfocussed—and in a few minutes, she stepped back onto the beach and signalled to Reo.

"It's still just one colour?" he asked when he joined her.

"Yes, so a single Mage." She pointed at a path that led between two palm trees. "We'll go that way. I'll clear the mage mist, and you can mark the path." She looked up at him. The sun had set but it was still light enough for her to see his face. Once they were in the trees, mage mist would light her way but Reo wouldn't be able to see much. "It's possible that simply stepping into the mist will get us to Chal faster." While mad, Santos had created multiple relocation spells: perhaps this Mage had as well.

"No. We're here to find out what happened to Chal," Reo said. "Not follow him into danger."

"You're right, we don't want that," Kara agreed. And besides, a relocation spell could send them out to sea. She looked around. Had that happened to Chal? Had he stepped into a patch of mage mist and been sent to the middle of the ocean? She stared out along the beach. His body hadn't washed ashore here nor had they seen anything on their trip around the island. She had to assume that he was somewhere on this island. Alive.

Kara walked slowly along the path, making sure all traces of mage mist were cleared not only from the trail, but from a foot on either side of it, too. Every dozen or so steps, Reo had her wait while he cut an arrow, pointing in the direction they were travelling.

It was slow, but safe. The moon was high in the sky when they reached a campsite.

"Chal?" Kara called as she rushed into the small clearing. "Chal?"

"He hasn't been here in a long time," Reo said. He set one boot into the remains of a fire and toed aside a charred log. "Maybe weeks. It looks like he only had a few fires."

"It's a pretty clear spot," Kara said. "There's not a lot of mage mist. That must be why he chose it." She brushed at some mist that clung to a nearby tree, and it dissipated.

"We can stop here for a rest," Reo said. "If you want."

"Let's keep going." She took a sip from her waterskin and handed it to Reo. "I'm looking for the area blanketed with the most mage mist, and that will be easier for me to see while it's still dark."

"The most?" Reo asked as he handed the waterskin back to her. "Is that safe?"

"Probably not," Kara replied. "So stay close. But Chal wouldn't have known he was dealing with a mad mage. He would have headed for the area with the most spells, assuming that the Mage had been using magic with a purpose. Creating a place to live, for example, and not just generating random spells." She studied the mage mist before choosing a direction. "This way. Mark the trail so that they know we went this way."

She brushed mage mist away as she walked, pausing every so often while Reo marked their path.

"At least Chal had all his supplies with him," Kara said. She was trying to hold out hope that the Seyoyan was alive. "Nothing was at either the boat or his camp."

"Yes," Reo agreed. "He should still have food for another week or so." He bumped into her when she paused to study the mage mist that covered the path. "Sorry." He removed the hand that had found its way to her shoulder.

"Leave it," Kara said. "Your hand. Mage mist is really thick here and you need to be within my . . . I'm not sure what to call it. My protective sphere?"

"All right." Reo's hand returned to her shoulder, and she felt him move closer to her.

A bird called from nearby—a high pitched trill—and Kara tensed.

"None of the animals on the island are a danger to us," Reo said into her ear. "According to Javan."

"Thanks, I didn't even think to ask." So it was just Mages they had to worry about. Or a single Mage who was not in his right mind.

Kara led the way along the faint path. Up ahead, mage mist rose above the palm trees, but it wasn't until they stepped out from beneath the trees that she saw the rock face.

Thirty feet high, mage mist swirled thickly at the bottom of it, but thinned out until only a few wisps reached the top. She peered up: bushes and grass lined the ledge above.

"It's a cliff," she said to Reo. "The mage mist thickens and then stops here." She took a few steps closer, clearing mage mist away so that she could see past it to the rocks underneath.

Crevasses and cracks lined the rock and stones that had probably fallen from the cliff littered the base. And there—where the mist was thickest—was that a . . . ? "There's a cave," she said, approaching it. "I can't see where it goes, but mage mist is really dense here." She went to take another step, but Reo's hand on her shoulder stopped her.

"We should wait for daylight," he said. "And the sailors."

"I can clear it of mage mist," Kara said. "At the very least."

"Don't go inside," Reo said. "We have no idea what might be hiding there. But I think we can assume that Chal went in and didn't come out. Remember, we are here to rescue him, not share his fate."

"Yes, of course, you're right."

It took her half an hour to clear all of the mage mist from the opening of the cave. Unlike the gentle ripples of mist they'd encountered along the path, some of this mist—some of the *spells*—had direction and purpose. Kara still didn't sense any evil or malicious intent but it was much more difficult to remove actual spells than the unfocused mage mist that blanketed the rest of the island.

"That's the last," she said as she stepped back from the rock face. Firelight flickered across the cracked and lined surface, creating shadows.

"Tea is ready," Reo said. "And soup."

She turned to see him sitting by a small fire, stirring a pot with a tree branch. She crossed the small clearing and sat down with a sigh. Now that she'd stopped moving, she realized that she was exhausted. Gratefully, she accepted a mug. She leaned over it— fish soup—and blew on it before taking a sip.

"Thank you." She put the mug down beside her and stared into the fire. "We must be close to finding him." She didn't say that she was afraid of finding Chal: that this mage mist—these actual spells—had her worried that the Mage wasn't as mad as Santos had been; that he was capable of creating spells with purpose. And that one of those spells might have hurt or killed their friend.

"We'll find him once it's daylight," Reo said, and she was grateful for his confidence. "And he'll be fine." Reo drained his own soup, rinsed the mug out, and poured something else into it. "Let me know when you're ready for tea."

Kara picked up her soup. It had cooled so she took a big gulp, finishing it in three swallows. She handed her mug to Reo, who rinsed it before pouring tea and handing it back to her.

"When you're done, try to get some sleep," he said. "You did all the work tonight so I'll keep watch. My guess is that we'll have four, maybe five hours before the sailors arrive."

"Thank you," she said again. She was too tired to argue with him, and besides, Reo was right. She had used her talent enough that she was exhausted, and if she expected to be able to do more of the same in a few hours, she needed some rest.

Her tea was only half finished when she spread her cloak in front of the fire and lay down on it, her head pillowed on her arm. As she hovered between being awake and asleep, she savoured how safe she felt with Reo watching over her; and how much she wanted him to do that—always.

THE EXIT WAS right . . . here. He reached out to where he thought the passageway would be—where it *should* be—but his hand found nothing but rough rock walls.

"There's no way out."

He turned in the direction of the voice. "I need to make one?" he asked tentatively.

"Yes. Using magic."

The speaker was illuminated by a mage light that sat in the middle of a dirt path. He had dark skin and a head of white braids. Had he done that to him or had the other man always been dark?

"We've met before," he said to his companion. "But I don't remember when."

"At least you remember something," his companion said. "You don't always. Now try to remember this: do not go to sleep. Don't nap, don't lie down, and do not sleep. Not unless you want us both to die in this cave."

"I don't want to die," he said. "But I've spent most of my time in caves." How did he know that? And where were the other caves he'd spent time in? Where was this one?

"Here, drink some water." His companion handed him a waterskin. "There's no food left, though."

"Thank you." He drank some water and handed the waterskin back to his companion. "You're very kind." He was certain that his companion would have shared his food if he'd had any. Had he already shared his food? Was that why there was none left?

"Kind, sure," his companion said.

He seemed upset—was he angry at him? Had he done something to make him angry? Then he knew. "It's my fault. If we die in this cave, it's my fault." If that was the case, he couldn't very well blame the man for being angry. And still, he had been kind.

"Not your fault," his companion said. "Someone did something to you—something that I think makes you create spells that you don't mean to."

"How do you know? That someone did something to me?"

"I can see it. There's a spell around your head—a dark-grey spell." His companion laughed, and it made him wonder if he was completely well. "I haven't actually seen your face because there's such a dense spell covering you."

"Oh." He felt a jolt of recognition. Someone *had* done something to him. It was just . . . beyond his ability to remember. "Did I deserve it?" he wondered out loud. "Did I do something so terrible that I deserve to be in a cave?" And if he had done something that terrible maybe he didn't want to remember?

"I don't see how anyone could deserve what you've been put through," his companion said. "And I sure don't deserve it but it seems I'm to share your fate."

"That does not seem fair." His head hurt and he was tired. He needed to think about this—think about what he should do.

"Do not go to sleep!" his companion yelled.

But it was too late. For some reason, thinking about who had done this to him made him tired—too tired to keep his eyes open. He sank to the ground—and into a deep sleep—despite the shouts of his companion.

"DID YOU HEAR that?"

Kara woke with a start and sat up. The fire still burned, but she no longer needed the light from it to see. She stared at Reo, who sat poised on a rock, an intent look on his face.

"Hear what?" she whispered.

Reo shook his head. "I thought I heard someone shouting." He gestured towards the mouth of the cave. "From there." He got up and took a few steps towards the mouth of the cave. "But I don't hear anything now."

"But shouting?" Kara asked. "You're certain your heard someone shouting?" It had to be Chal. He was alive. Was he in the cave?

"Not certain, no," Reo said. "It could be wishful thinking." He sat back down by the fire. "I've made tea. Since you're awake, I'll head down the trail and see if the sailors have come ashore yet."

"All right." Reo left, and Kara poured some tea and sipped it as she stared at the mouth of the cave. What if it was Chal? What if he'd yelled because he was in trouble?

She got up and leaned over to grab her pack to look for journey bread. When she straightened, she stared at the cave. Two steps took her to the mouth of it, and she peered inside.

It was dark, which mean that there was no mage mist. It would be safe for her to investigate, wouldn't it? She looked behind her at the trail Reo had taken. He wouldn't be happy, but she'd just take a few steps into the cave. There might be an outcrop or bend in the tunnel that was hiding mage mist—she could just remove any that she found and make it safe for everyone.

She slung her pack over her shoulder and took a tentative step into the cave, then another. She was in total darkness now, for the first time since she'd stepped onto this island. She took another step and still there was no mage mist.

She reached out to touch the wall of the cave. The rock was cool and dry beneath her hand. She looked back outside: the campfire still burned and Reo hadn't yet returned. Just one more step.

Air swooshed past her and suddenly she was surrounded by mage mist so dense she could hardly see her arm in front of her.

She spun around—there was no sign of the campfire—no sign of the mouth to the cave. All she could see was this swirling mass of mage mist. Automatically she started waving her hands, dispersing the magic until it was thin enough to see through, concentrating on making it disappear until all of the mage mist was gone.

"Who's there?" someone called.

"Chal?" Kara replied. "Is that you?" A light was lifted shoulder high, and she saw Chal Honess. "Thank Gyda, you're all right," Kara said. She rushed to his side. He looked unhurt, but then he frowned.

"Kara," Chal said and sighed. "No matter how glad I am to see you, I wish you weren't here."

Chapter Five

Voices woke him up. "Who's there?" he called out. He got up and started walking towards the voices. As he passed a rock wall, he frowned. Wasn't something supposed to be there?

"Who's there?" he called again.

"Just me," someone said. "And a friend."

A mage light sat on the floor of the cave, and a dark man with white braids was staring at him. Beside him was another man with paler skin and dark hair . . . something about this second man—no, it was a woman—was familiar.

"I know you!" he said to the woman. "I know you!" He concentrated, trying to remember how he knew her, where he'd seen her, but he couldn't. He slapped his palm against his forehead. "You're her, you're her, but I can't remember!"

"We've never met," the woman replied. "I would remember you."

"Would you?" he asked. "Remember? Because I can't. I should be able to, but I can't." He stared at her. She was young—younger than she should be, but he had no idea why he thought that. "Do you know where we are?"

"Yes," she replied. "We're in a cave."

"Do you know where the exit is? There's supposed to be a way out." He looked over his shoulder. "This way, I think." He started to walk away from the light and his two companions. The exit should be here. As he stood staring at the wall, he yawned, suddenly overcome with fatigue. He'd look for the door later, after he'd slept. Then he would be refreshed. He lay down on the dirt floor and fell asleep.

"HE'LL WAKE UP in an hour or two," Chal said. "And he'll have forgotten everything that just happened. I'm assuming it's because of the spell wrapped around his head."

"The curse," Kara replied. "Or more likely multiple curses. That's what he did to Santos. Multiple spells layered on top of each other."

"You know who did this."

"Valerio Valendi." She sighed. "The same man who cursed Santos. But why this man? Who is he?"

"I have no idea," Chal replied. "And neither does he, although he seemed to recognize you, for some reason."

"I've never met him," Kara said. "There's only one reason why I would look familiar *and* why he would have been cursed by Valendi: he must know my mother." This meant that this Mage—whoever he was—sane or mad, couldn't be trusted.

"I can't offer you any food," Chal said. "But there's a spring at the far end of the cave. I hope you have some great plan to get us out of here. I'm afraid that the exit our Mage friend keeps talking about does not exist."

"I have some supplies," Kara said, grateful that she'd had her bag with her. She pulled out some journey bread and handed it to Chal.

"Thank you." He took a bite and started chewing. "Although I'm not sure it won't just delay the inevitable."

"But there was an opening," Kara said. "At least there was a way in, so there must be a way out."

"With magic, yes," Chal agreed. He licked a few crumbs off his fingers. "Which we need our Mage friend for. But he never stays awake long enough to remember how to do it."

"Then I'll have to remove the curses," Kara said. "Just as I did with Santos." Which had taken her weeks, not the handful of days they had until the food she'd brought was gone. "And Reo is outside, along with Sif and Javan. They'll find a way to help us."

"As long as they don't all end up in here *with* us," Chal said. He reached over and picked up the mage light. "Come on, when he's asleep he's impossible to wake. This is as good a time as any to take a look at those curses."

Kara followed Chal the few steps to where the Mage lay sleeping. She peered down at the mass of mage mist that blanketed his head. The closer she got the more aware she was of the malice and hate that was infused into the spells. A few ropey strands were as thick as her wrist but many were thin wisps.

Tentatively she reached a hand towards the Mage's head. Mage mist retreated as her fingers got closer. The mage whimpered and she pulled her hand away. She backed away and straightened, looking at Chal, who'd been hovering over her shoulder.

"It will take time," she said. "But none of the spells look worse than the ones Santos was cursed with." She hoped. She might have some experience but it wasn't as though she was an expert on removing curses. She blew out a breath. She *was* the only one she knew of who'd had any success doing it.

"Do you need him to be awake?" Chal asked. "Can't you just do it now, while he's asleep?"

"I'm not sure." She'd only ever removed curses from Santos with his permission and while he was awake and sane. "Santos would tell me what curses caused him pain while I was trying to remove them." She didn't mention that one curse would have killed Santos if he hadn't been able to show her how it had been created. "And that was often helpful." She looked down at the sleeping mage. "So, I think it best if I can remove them from him while he's awake and alert." At the very least she needed to have him agree to let her meddle with whatever had been done to him. He might not be capable of creating a way out of the cave, but that didn't mean he couldn't cast a spell that made their situation worse.

"He'll be up soon enough," Chal said. "Maybe you can figure out which spell is making him sleep. If he can stay awake long enough he might have time to remember how to do magic and get us out of here."

"I WAS EXPECTING to see Javan Losi," Chal said. They were sitting just past the bend in the tunnel, away from where the Mage slept. "I thought he'd be the one I died with; that they'd send him to find me and he'd get trapped in here with me." He picked up a pebble and threw it into the darkness. "Or that he'd find me dead and he'd be next."

"They did ask him," Kara said. "But he chose to fetch me. He didn't think it made sense to send someone with lesser a talent to try to save you."

"Smart of him," Chal said. "Too bad it didn't actually work out for me. Or you."

"We're not going to die," Kara said. "Reo will bring Santos if he has to."

"Will he come? Santos. Will he come?"

"Yes," Kara said. "He'll come. He'll need to strengthen the spells around his estate, but he'll come." As long as someone sailed to Old Rillidi and convinced him to come. That meant Reo, Sif, and Javan had to realize what had happened and that Santos was needed. And the small amount of food she had with her got them all to the day when Santos arrived.

"Have you seen the exit?" a tremulous voice asked. "Who's out there?"

"He's awake," Chal said. "Do you mind if I give him something to eat and drink before you talk to him? We have little chance to have him create a spell if he's too weak to do magic."

"Go ahead." Kara handed him another portion of travel bread.

Chal took that, his waterskin, and the mage light to where the Mage had been sleeping. She heard them have a low conversation, and then a few moments later, the mage light came towards her.

"I know you," the Mage said. "Or I should. Do you know me?"

"I think you know my mother," Kara said. "Her name is Arabella."

"Arabella, Arabella, Arabella," the Mage whispered. He frowned. "It's as familiar and unfamiliar as anything is to me." He sighed. "Have you seen the exit?"

"You need to make an exit," Chal said. "But you've forgotten how. Kara is going to help you remember by removing the spells that keep you from remembering. Is that all right with you?"

"Yes. I've forgotten so much, haven't I?" the Mage said. "Will it hurt? Removing spells so I can remember?"

"It might at times," Kara replied. At least it had for Santos, a few times. "But probably not in the beginning." She raised a hand, and the Mage flinched and she frowned. That was not the reaction a powerful Mage would have, was it? As though he expected be struck?

"I need you to relax," she continued. "And tell me what you feel."

The Mage nodded as her hand crept closer to him. She concentrated on a thin fragment of mage mist, drawing it towards her. It swirled, untwisting from around his head, and she stepped away, pulling the trailing spell with her.

"Someone hates me," the Mage said.

"Yes," Kara agreed. She flicked her hand, and the spell twisted and faded until it was gone. "Do you remember why?"

"I was in love once," the Mage whispered. Then he yawned. "So tired." He yawned again. "Must sleep."

Kara was about to grab his arm when Chal stopped her, shaking his head.

"It won't work," Chal said. "I've found it impossible to make him stay awake, no matter what I do."

The Mage didn't look at either of them as he shuffled back to where he'd been sleeping earlier.

"Probably part of the curse." Kara ran a hand through her hair and sat down with her back against the wall. "When he wakes we'll see what changes removing that spell had on him."

Chal joined her. "And that's what you did with Santos? Removed a spell and then tried to figure out what the spell had been doing to him?"

"Yes. But with Santos it was more complicated. He'd been cursed for years and he'd also had other Mages try to help using even more spells. He had layers upon layers of spells—from many different Mages. But the dark-grey ones—the ones created by Valendi? I always knew they were the dangerous spells even though at the time I couldn't sense it."

"But you can sense that now?" Chal asked. "Which are the bad spells?"

"Yes. And with this Mage they're all dangerous—they're all curses." She paused. "He was right, when he said that someone hates him. Although it's past tense, since Valerio Valendi is dead." And even in death he was causing harm and grief. Kara had to wonder why her mother had ever thought it a good idea to align herself with Valendi enough to have his child.

"Oh," she said. "I almost forgot. Reo thought he heard

shouting. That's why I entered the cave. I was worried that if you were alive, you were shouting because you were in danger."

"Yes." Chal stood up. "Right before you arrived. I was shouting at our friend to stay awake. Not that it did any good." He picked up the mage light and went a few paces to the right. "You came in here." He peered down at the rocky ground. "I marked the spot." He slapped a hand on the wall beside him. "Reo!" he called. "Reo!"

Kara joined him and pressed her ear against the wall. "Reo!" she shouted, willing him to answer. "Reo!" She sighed when she didn't hear a response.

"He might not be back yet," she said. "He was going to meet the sailors and lead them to the cave. We should try calling out every hour or so." She sat down again. Their best chance was for her to remove the curses from the Mage. That would make him sane, although not necessarily a friend. But if Valerio Valendi had hated him, could she trust him? And wouldn't he want out of here too, even if he was an enemy?

Chal slid down to sit beside her. He took out a waterskin and offered it to her. She took a couple of swallows and handed it back to him. The water was cool, with a slight metallic taste to it.

"How long have I been here?" Chal asked. "I tried to keep track at first but then I gave up. When the Mage sleeps I try to sleep so I can be awake when he's awake." He shrugged. "I've been trying to get him to tell me how he creates spells so I can tell him how to do it when he wakes up."

"Any luck?"

"Some." He toed the mage light. "Enough to make a light. This is the second one he's created. It proves to him that he can do magic."

"I wonder who he is," Kara mused. "He must be fairly powerful. Valerio Valendi wouldn't waste his time—risk his position—by cursing a low-level Mage." Or maybe he would. He'd deliberately sent Osten to live with a man who did terrible things to children: she didn't believe Valendi hadn't known what would happen to her brother. A man mean-spirited enough to do that would be spiteful enough to harm another Mage no matter how insignificant he was.

HIS NECK WAS sore. He rolled over, wondering what in Gyda's

name he was sleeping on that was so hard. He felt rocks and dirt under his hand. He must have fallen asleep and slid off the bench again. But why had no one woken him up?

He opened his eyes and attempted to stand, his hand searching for—and not finding—the table.

"Wald?" he called. "Are you there?" Surely his counterpart in the workroom had noticed him lying on the floor. "Wald?"

"You're awake," someone said. A mage light was raised over him, and he squinted against its glare.

"Awake, yes. Who are you?"

"Chal," the man said. "Who are you?"

"I'm . . ." His name was on the tip of his tongue. Why couldn't he say it? Why couldn't he remember it?"

"Who's Wald?" a woman asked. She drifted into the light and he gasped.

"I never thought I'd see you again," he whispered. His love—his only love—and she was here. Which was where? He yawned. He was so tired. He didn't want to sleep, but he was so tired. "Don't leave me," he managed to say before his head drooped to his chest. He started to topple over but someone—his love!—gently helped him down to the floor.

"That was definitely an improvement," Chal said. He stared down at the Mage. "He'll be asleep for an hour or so, is my guess."

Kara followed Chal back to where she'd entered the cave. "He thinks he knows me. And he knows someone named Wald. That might help when he wakes next time."

"He's usually looking for the exit," Chal said. "I hope that doesn't mean he's forgotten that we're stuck in this cave."

"If it's anything like Santos' madness then he might get worse before he gets better." Or she might kill him while trying to help him. She placed a hand on the wall. "This is where I came in?"

"Yes. Reo!" Chal called. "Reo!"

Kara put her hand up and he stopped calling out. She put her head against the wall. Was that banging? Was someone deliberately banging on the cave wall? She stepped away and searched the ground. She picked up a rock and smashed it against the wall—once, twice, three times. Dirt crumbled to the floor, and her hand tingled from the impact.

She leaned her head against the wall. There! Three distinct

sounds. "I think Reo's found the other side of our cave," she said.

"Oh no!" Chal said. "He'll end up in here with us!" He grabbed the rock from Kara's hand and started tapping out a complicated pattern.

"No, he won't," Kara said. "I destroyed the spell when I came in."

Chal stopped banging on the wall and looked at her. "You did?" He smiled. "We may have two ways of getting out then." He pressed his ear to the rock and Kara copied him.

She heard rapid tapping from the other side of the wall. When it stopped, Chal started pounding on the wall again.

"I told Reo we're both alive," Chal said. "And that he should try to dig us out from that side."

"You talked to him?" Kara asked. "By hitting a rock against the cave wall?"

"It's a Warrior method of communicating," Chal said. "They also have a series of hand signals." He shrugged. "I'm not sure I'm supposed to know them—and I'm certain I'm not supposed to share that knowledge—but Reo taught them to me."

"Thank Gyda," Kara said, grateful that they didn't have to rely on her efforts with the mad mage to save themselves. The ship would have tools to dig through the rock, wouldn't they? "And you can ask Reo to send for Santos."

"If needed. I think we'll see what the sailors can do." He turned to her. "I didn't have a lot of hope, not even when you arrived. But now that I know Reo is out there? For the first time in weeks, I feel like I—like we—are going to get out of here."

"Wald?" the Mage called out from down the hall. "Is that you? What's happening?"

"I'll check on him," Kara said. She still wanted to help. Besides, a powerful Mage not in control of his wits or his magic was dangerous.

"Wald's not here," Kara said as she reached the still prone form. Mage mist swirled around him as though it was reacting to his troubled emotions.

"Not here?" the Mage asked. "Why? Aren't we in the workroom?" He looked up at her and his eyes widened. "My love. You shouldn't be here! Why are you back? Do I need to pay them more to keep you out of here?"

"I'm here to see you," Kara replied. She knelt down beside

him. He had to be talking about her mother—there was no one else it could be. But he kept calling her his love. Had her mother loved this man before she met Val—?

She sat back on her heels. That was it; that was why he'd been cursed.

Did her mother know? Did she know that this Mage—this man who loved her—who from the sounds of it had paid someone in order to help her—had been cursed by the man who had fathered her child? Would Arabella Fonti even care? Or had this Mage simply been another man she used to get what she wanted?

"To see me?" the Mage smiled. "That's very kind of you. And not required." He sat up and took her hand. "But it is nice to see you."

"I came to help," Kara said. "Will you let me help?"

The Mage nodded. "But I am so tired." His eyes drooped but he stayed upright.

Kara stood and walked around him, studying the mage mist— the dark-grey curses that Valerio Valendi had inflicted on him. There—she poked a thick rope of mist that didn't seem to be connected to anything else. The Mage shivered but didn't open his eyes.

Concentrating on the spell, Kara mentally pulled at it while slowly drawing her finger away. The mist seemed to stretch and then it broke. The Mage cried out and toppled over, but the spell clung to her finger, and Kara couldn't risk stopping what she was doing to help him. Instead, she stepped away from him, praying that he hadn't been too badly hurt, the spell trailing her.

She suppressed a shiver—she thought that this spell had been created to cause pain—and pointed her finger to the ground. The spell slowly sank into the dirt. When it was gone, she rubbed her hand on her trousers, trying to rid herself of the terrible intent of the spell.

"Even I could feel the hate in that spell," Chal said from behind her. "Is he all right?" He knelt beside the Mage and leaned over him. "He's breathing."

Kara sighed. "That's something." She bent down and stared at the remaining spells. She whisked away a few loose strands that had been hidden by the spell she'd just removed. "Hopefully he'll be more himself when he wakes." She stood and Chal rose too.

"He knows my mother," she said. "Loves her. I think that's

why Valendi cursed him. He couldn't let my mother have someone who loved her."

"Valendi was jealous?" Chal asked. "Winning her wasn't enough for him so he had to curse the man he'd won her from?"

"It was probably more because he didn't want my mother to have anyone she could trust," Kara said. She didn't think Valerio Valendi had been capable of loving anyone enough to be jealous.

"Santos told me," she continued, "that he was deliberately cursed so that he had lucid periods when he knew what had been done to him. That was part of Valendi's vengeance—for Santos to know he was cursed and realize that he had no way to remove them." She paused. Some days she still struggled with the fact that she'd killed Valerio Valendi, but he had been a terrible person. "And Santos had been his mentor."

HE WOKE UP in the dark—not the workroom. He knew that by the way the air smelled. Voices drifted to him—a woman and a man—and he wondered why he wasn't alone after being banished to this island.

He sat up and rubbed his head. There was a lump on it—had he fallen? He didn't remember falling, but there was so much he didn't remember.

A faint light threw shadows on the wall from the direction the voices were coming from. It was a mage light, not the flickering of a flame. He drew some power and created a second light and let it hover in the air near his head. He'd always been good at lights, although more difficult spells were beyond him. That was why he'd been assigned to the workroom. He had power, but he wasn't able to focus it. And without political or family allies, Mage Guild had determined his life and his fate.

"There's a light," a woman exclaimed. "He must be awake."

He saw her silhouette first, and for a moment his heart was in his throat—then she stepped out of the dim passage and into the glare of his mage light. It wasn't her, although there was much about her that reminded him of his love. But she was young, this one, not much more than a girl.

"How do you feel?" she asked.

"Fine." He touched his head again. Was he ill?

"You hit your head," she said. "When I . . . tried to help you."

"Is he better?" A man loomed over the girl—a Seyoyan. He

hadn't met that many of the dark-skinned islanders, but he wasn't surprised to see one. He had been banished to Seyoya after all.

"Have I been ill?" he asked. Both of his companions seemed to think he had been, but he couldn't remember . . . anything really, after being told he was being banished. He didn't even know why he'd been sent away.

"Yes," the girl said. "And someone did it deliberately. Do you remember?"

"No, not really." He tried to concentrate but shook his head. He couldn't remember and trying to was giving him a headache.

"Do you know where you are?" the Seyoyan asked.

"Yes. I'm in Seyoya," he replied. "I've been banished." He rubbed the lump on his head. How had he hit his head?

"My name is Kara," the girl said. "What's yours?"

"I'm . . ." he frowned. He had a name—everyone had a name. "My name is . . ." Why couldn't he remember his name?

"You were asking for someone called Wald," the Seyoyan said. "Is that you?"

"No, Wald is . . ." He knew the name—he could practically see Wald—but he couldn't describe him. Or say how he knew him.

"How about Arabella Fonti," the girl—Kara—said.

"My love," he said. *Her* he could picture—*her* he remembered. Beautiful, cold, and calculating. But he loved her—even though he knew she'd only use him—knew she'd set him aside as soon as someone more useful came along. But he loved her anyway.

"She's my mother," Kara said.

"That's why you remind me of her." He had a feeling he should be shocked that his Arabella had an almost-grown daughter—but he wasn't. His love had so many secrets—including things she'd wanted to keep from herself.

"I can help you," Kara said. "If you'll let me."

"I hear something," the Seyoyan said. He rushed down the hall and out of sight. "I think they're digging," he called back to them.

"Our friends," Kara said. "They're coming to get us. But I still want to help you, if I can."

"All right, but can we do it later?" He was tired. Was that from hitting his head? "I need to sleep." He yawned and lay down without even waiting for her reply. As he drifted off, he heard her retreating footsteps.

KARA PUSHED HER hair from her face. She and Chal had been sitting by the wall of the cave for hours. The sounds of digging, or pickaxing, or whatever they were doing to get through the rock continued, but it didn't seem any closer.

"What does a pickaxe look like?" she asked.

"You're the one from a mountain villa," Chal said. "Haven't you seen one?"

"My villa didn't mine," Kara said. "And anyway, I was Mage Guild. I wouldn't have been exposed to miners or their tools— they would be Masons, I didn't have any reason to deal with them."

"Even in a small villa the guilds lived apart?" Chal shook his head. "I never believed that the way Rillidi was laid out, each guild with its own island, separate from the other guilds, was the rule. In Seyoya we all live together and are friends with each other. Tregella is so confusing."

"Do you still think I could make a living there?" she asked. "In Seyoya? Teaching about the guilds? Sif said he thought I could."

"He's right. Especially when you add your talent for undoing magic spells. For unmagic."

"Unmagic," Kara repeated. "That's a good name for it." And that skill—unmagic—was what everyone wanted from her. And why people like her mother and Primus Rorik wanted her dead. But what would happen to Santos' agreement with Warrior Guild if she didn't return? Would they make Reo go back to the guild? Force him to be an Assassin again? He would hate that. *She* would hate that.

And they could. Santos said that the terms of the contract were that as long as she did it to the best of her abilities; as long as she tried, the contract was valid. But that meant that if she stopped trying, if she left Old Rillidi, the contract would no longer be valid.

She blew out a breath. It had seemed so easy when she'd agreed to it: a little of her time and talent for Reo's freedom.

"I'm going to check on the Mage," Kara said as she got to her feet. She picked up the waterskin and took it with her.

He was still sleeping, this nameless Mage who loved her mother: and who had been cursed by her mother's lover.

The mage light still hovered near his shoulder. Grey-black

mage mist circled his head. It was thinner than it had been. There were a few wispy strands so she waved them away. Now there were just a couple of thicker bands.

She felt odd staring at the Mage while he slept; she would have preferred him to be awake for this, but he had agreed to let her help him. She wanted to remove all of the curses before Reo and the sailors broke through the wall. If the Mage and she went their separate ways, he would be cursed for the rest of his life. She didn't want that and was certain he wouldn't either.

She could see that one of the main curses had multiple, smaller spells attached to it. If she got rid of them, the large one might be less focused. That would probably make it easier—and less dangerous—to remove.

She reached her hand towards the spells, holding it a few inches from the Mage's head. She concentrated on the mage mist; on willing it to come to her.

A ribbon of mage mist snaked out from the swirling mass and headed to her index finger. When it touched her, she shivered. The mist felt damp, and she could feel the terrible intent of the spell. She stretched her fingers apart and the mist crossed her palm and travelled the length of her little finger. She reached down until her little finger touched the dirt floor. The mage mist pooled there for a moment before slowly fading to nothing.

The Mage mumbled something and waved a hand towards his head, but he didn't wake.

The spell continued to unspool from around his head and travel along her finger to the ground. Once the smaller spells were gone the larger spell started to tighten around the Mage's neck.

"No, you don't." Kara shoved her hand into the mist focusing all her will on it, forcing the mist to weaken and *come away*. Suddenly, it snapped apart, and the mage mist—the spell—flew towards the wall. It sparked and hissed when it hit the rock, startling her.

"What was that?" Chal rushed around the corner. "Are you all right?"

Kara, slumped over the Mage, lifted her head. "I'm fine. We're both fine."

The Mage shifted in sleep. He had only one major spell left circling his head. Kara waved a few straggling wisps away and stared down at him.

"I can see his face now," she said. "He looks very . . . ordinary."

"Most of us do," Chal replied. "Do you think he can make a way out now? It's not that I don't appreciate what Reo's doing out there, but we have no idea how thick the rock here is. It could take weeks for them to get through."

"Maybe he's ready to do magic," Kara said. "Let's hope."

Chapter Six

He knew where he was, but he still didn't know *who* he was. He was trapped in a cave with a Seyoyan and Arabella's daughter.

That almost made him think he was dreaming—except that it made perfect sense. The child explained Arabella Fonti's age when she'd arrived on Mage Guild Island: why she was powerful but untrained at an age when most Mages were well into their Journeyman schooling.

She'd been assigned to the workroom, like him, and he'd immediately been smitten. She'd allowed his attentions—he'd never been under the illusion that she loved him—but in that workroom—in that hopeless life—loving her, being able to see her every day—was enough.

And even better, he'd been the one to help her escape that life.

He'd been an Apprentice once, to a Mage of middling power. He'd never been able to manage his power, but the Mage had liked him. So he'd convinced—and paid—that Mage to take on Arabella as his student.

She'd been grateful—grateful enough that she'd bedded him—and he'd had that memory to help him get through all of the years in the workroom.

And he'd kept track of her, when he could. She'd soon outgrown his old mentor and had acquired a new master. Rumours said that she'd bed anyone who could teach her how to use her magic; how to harness her abilities.

He'd always assumed the rumours were true, and he didn't blame her. He'd always known she'd use whatever gifts she had in order to lift herself up. Anyone would—anyone *should*. Anything was better than the half-life of a workroom.

He sat up. His head felt clearer than he could remember, but all he seemed to be doing was remembering. Except his name: he still didn't know who he was. Or why he'd been banished to Seyoya. He must have come to this island by ship, but he would swear he'd never been on one in his life. He'd only been on a boat once: his master had taken him below the island and they'd floated around for a few minutes. That was before his master knew he was hopeless: before he realized that he'd never be able to control his magic.

"You're awake." It was the girl—Kara Fonti—the daughter of the woman he loved.

"Yes. You said you could help me. Did you?"

"Yes. I hope you're not angry."

"No, thank you." He patted his head. "I feel much better. And I can remember things—mostly about your mother—although I still can't remember my own name." He sighed. Perhaps that was because he had never been important, not even to himself. Arabella Fonti, on the other hand, had become very important.

"You may never remember everything," Kara said. "At least the other Mage I helped in this same way has yet to regain all of his memories."

"Another Mage was like me? Did the same thing happen to that Mage?"

"He was cursed, yes," Kara said. "By Valerio Valendi, just as you were."

"Cursed!" He was shocked. That would be grounds for death, if caught. "The Mage Guild Secundus cursed me. Why? Do you know?"

"Because he could," Kara replied. "My guess is that he learned of you—maybe from my mother—and decided to hurt you. Perhaps to hurt her or to make sure she had no one she could trust, or even to prove to her that he wasn't above being so petty and mean." She shrugged.

"Arabella and Valerio Valendi, yes." He nodded. As soon as the girl said the name, he remembered: his Arabella had attached herself to the Mage Guild Secundus. Dangerous, is what he'd thought at the time. And then he'd . . . then he'd what? "Then I suppose it was worthless. Arabella never cared about me."

"Or me," Kara said. "She doesn't even like to acknowledge that she's my mother."

"Has Mage Secundus Valendi tried to hurt her through you?" Valendi was ruthless—he'd seen the man kill a worker for not giving up his chair to him. The worker had been old and practically crippled, but that hadn't mattered to Valerio Valendi. That's why he'd . . . what? Had he done something to try to protect Arabella? Something that attracted Valendi's attention? "He'll try again if he has a chance."

"Valendi's dead, so he doesn't matter anymore. My mother is Mage Guild Secundus now."

He looked up at her in shock. His Arabella had risen to the second highest level of Mage Guild. And he'd helped her take that first step. He was very proud of his love. "She must be so happy." Even as he said the word, he knew Arabella wouldn't be happy. Satisfied, yes, pleased even, but happy? He thought that feeling was beyond her—just as love was.

"I'm not sure—"

There was a loud rumble and the ground shook. He shielded his head with his hands as pebbles and dust rained down on him from the ceiling. When he looked up, Kara had gone.

"WHAT HAPPENED?" KARA asked as she rounded the corner. Chal stood staring at the wall. "Did they break through?"

"No." Chal turned to her, a horrified look on his face. "I think there was a cave-in."

"What? How?" A cave-in? Had Reo been there? Was he hurt? She leaned against the wall, pleading with Gyda to keep him safe.

Dust filtered down from the rock ceiling above her, and she coughed.

"Can you tap on the wall and see if they're all right?" she asked Chal. When she turned to look at him, his eyes were sad.

"I'll try." He picked up the rock he'd used before and hit it against the wall three times, paused then hit it another two times.

With her eyes closed, Kara pressed her ear to the wall. Was that—? No, there was nothing, no sounds coming through the rock. Just the earth settling on this side.

Chal struck the wall again and paused, but there was still no reply.

"It doesn't mean they were . . . caught in it," Chal said.

"It doesn't mean they weren't," she replied. And Reo would have been there—he would have been the first one to pick up a tool and start digging in the morning and the last one to put it down at night.

She stepped back from the wall, shaking her head. They'd need to try again later. She turned to find the Mage staring at her.

"Can you make a way out now?" Chal asked him. "You need to make an exit."

The Mage backed away, cowering. "I can't," he said, "I never could. That's why I was sent to the workroom: I have power but I could never direct it, never make it do what I wanted it to do." He leaned against the opposite wall, his head bowed.

"You have to try!" Chal said. "You have to!"

"You're saying that you've never been able to create spells?" Kara asked. It would explain his story about the workroom.

"Only mage lights," the Mage replied, not meeting her eyes. "I've never been able to create any other spells worth anything."

"But you did while you were mad," Chal said. "You created a way in here—or filled in an existing passage. How can you do something while you're cursed that you can't normally do? We should have left him mad, then at least he'd be willing to try to help us get out of here."

"You tried that," Kara said gently. The Mage walked away from them, rounding the bend until he was out of sight. "For weeks, you tried that. And it didn't work." She sighed. She was tired and trying very hard to not worry about Reo, and she didn't want to give in to the panic and anger that was gripping Chal. "We'll figure something out," she said to Chal. "Or they'll start digging us out again soon."

Sha sat down and stared at the rock wall in front of her. What was happening on the other side of the wall? Where was Reo? She closed her eyes, blinking back tears.

For all her thoughts about staying in Seyoya, she wasn't running away, especially not from Reo. She was trying to give him time to realize that he did care for her—or give herself time to get used to living with the possibility that he never would.

But in no way did she plan on being away from Old Rillidi—or

Reo—forever. And now with the thought that she might never see him again—that he might be dead—she knew she didn't want to be away from him. Not even for a few months.

Why hadn't she told him how she felt? Why had she thought it would be easier to simply leave instead of being honest with him?

The unnamed Mage was braver than she was. He readily admitted that he loved and that his love was not reciprocated. Did he wallow in self-pity? Did he distance himself from the one he loved? Did he run away from the pain of loving someone who didn't love him back?

No. He did his best to help her get what she wanted, and then he cheered all of her accomplishments after that. And he cherished the time he'd had with her.

He was self-less in his love. Kara knew her mother would never understand, never appreciate that she was loved in this way; nor would she realize how much she didn't deserve it.

But Reo did. Reo deserved to be happy, to get what he wanted out of life after not being allowed to hope for a life of his own. He had one now—at least he did if he was still alive—and he deserved to have a chance to live it.

Which meant that when they got out of this cave, she wouldn't run away: she would fulfill her obligations to Warrior Guild and make sure that Reo remained free. And she would tell him how she felt and not expect anything in return. And she would be happy for him. Even if he found happiness with someone else.

Chal sighed and wandered away, taking the mage light with him. The other light still glowed from beyond the bend where the Mage was.

Kara stood against the wall, with her ear pressed to it. She should look in on the Mage—maybe try to remove the last curse— but she felt she needed to be here in case someone—in case *Reo*— tried to communicate with them. For as much as they were worried about those on the outside, they would be just as worried for them in here.

Chal came back and stared at her.

"It's worse than we thought," he said. He held up the waterskin. "The cave-in has cut off the stream and this is all the water we have left."

Kara held the mage light up as she knelt and pushed the pile of rocks and stones aside. There was a damp spot, but water no longer trickled out from the crevice in the wall. She sat back on her heels.

"It may come back," she said. "But it may not." She ran a hand through her hair. They had water for a day, maybe, if they rationed it carefully. She looked over her shoulder at Chal, who was pacing the width of the cave.

"So that's it," Chal said. He sighed. He tore a strip off his shirt and handed it to her. "Leave this on the water. It might soak up a few drops. It might be enough to delay the inevitable for a day or so."

Kara shoved the fabric into the dirt. It was better than giving up, but whatever moisture collected in the scrap of cloth wouldn't save them.

She stood up and handed the mage light to Chal and headed down the passageway.

"Where are you going?" Chal called after her.

"To remove the final curse from the Mage," she said. "He might be our only hope."

"He can't do magic," Chal said from right behind her. The light he was holding made her shadow stretch out in front of her.

"I know. But he still *has* magic—he might be able to do something." Or she might be able to direct his magic, if he could create even an unfocussed spell. She'd used Valerio Valendi's magic against him, so she knew she could do it. And so she would, because she had to.

SOMEONE WAS SHAKING his shoulder.

"Wake up," a woman said.

He squinted up at her. His love! No, it was her daughter. He sat up.

"What is it, Kara?"

"I need to remove the last curse, and I think it's best if you stay awake while I do it." She leaned over him, the Seyoyan hovering behind her with a mage light in his hand.

"All right." Something had happened—had it? "The cave-in," he said. "There was a cave-in—it happened when they tried to tunnel in from the other side."

"Yes," Kara replied. "And it's diverted the stream. We'll be out of water soon so we need to get out of here. For that, you must be able to do magic. Which means that I have to remove the curse." She stared down at him so intently that he wanted to squirm away.

"But I can't do spells," he said. "It's hopeless." He couldn't do magic. That was the bane of his life—that he couldn't do magic. If he couldn't make himself do magic in order to stay out of the workroom another desperate situation wasn't going to change that. "I'll fail again. Like I always do."

"Not always."

He hadn't realized he'd spoken that out loud until she responded.

"You didn't fail my mother, did you?" Kara asked. "You helped her, and now you're going to help me." She waved a hand over his head. "Tell me if anything hurts."

He closed his eyes, trying to concentrate on what he was feeling. She was right—he hadn't failed Arabella—*he* was the reason she'd escaped the fate of the workroom. *Him.* He smiled. He hadn't thought of that, hadn't realized that he'd been successful in that one thing.

"Ow." A splitting headache sucked the breath from him. He lifted a hand to his head, but Kara brushed it away.

"Sorry," she said. "I need to see. Does that feel better?"

"Yes," he gasped. He still had a headache but it no longer felt like a vise was tightening around his head.

"All right. This might be bad."

Pain stabbed his temple, and a scream tore from his throat. He clutched his head and fell onto his side. He took a deep, shuddering breath—and then suddenly the pain was gone.

"Gyda that hurt!" He was weak, too weak to even lift his head, but he was alive. And he knew who he was. He lay there for a few moments before he opened his eyes.

"Dario Todaro," he said.

"What was that?" Kara leaned over him, and he looked into her relieved eyes. "Did you say something?"

He smiled and she smiled back, tentatively.

"My name. Dario Todaro." He closed his eyes. "I think it worked." He was so tired. "Whatever you did, I think it worked."

"HE'S ASLEEP," KARA said as she straightened and stood up. "I'm not surprised. It happened with Santos sometimes. He'd fall asleep right after I removed a particularly nasty curse."

"But he's alive," Chal said. "And I don't see any more mage mist around him."

"I've removed it all," Kara agreed. She was thankful that he was alive—she hadn't been certain but she'd thought the last spell she removed had been a killing spell. Well, she'd treated it as one, and the Mage had lived through the removal of it.

"And he knows his name," she continued. "Dario Todaro. Hopefully he won't sleep for very long and we can try to get out of here."

"You have a plan," Chal said as he led them away from where the Mage—Dario—was sleeping back to the wall they hoped to escape through.

"I have an idea for a plan," Kara said. "And no way to know if it will work or not. Whatever spells Dario can create—or the magic he uses to try to create them—I hope to manipulate to . . . I don't know, dig through the rock and make a tunnel."

"You can do that?"

"I hope so." She really had no idea if she could or not, but she couldn't think of anything else. "I know I can redirect spells, so even if that's all I can do, it should work." It *would* work—there was no other choice. Not unless Dario could suddenly create a spell that saved them all.

"If anyone can, you can," Chal said. He sat down with his back to the wall, and Kara joined him.

She appreciated his confidence when she wasn't feeling quite so certain. She'd need to convince Dario that he, too, could do what was required.

She sighed. It was still quiet; digging had not resumed so either everyone was dead—her heart constricted at the thought of Reo being gone—or it was no longer safe to dig there.

She pushed down her fear for Reo's safety—it wouldn't help her—and instead stared at the wall in front of her.

"You said that you knew the exact spot where I came in?" she asked Chal, who had been pressing his ear against the wall.

Head bent, Chal paced along the wall. "Right here." He pointed at a spot on the rock. "I made this mark just after you arrived." He met her eyes and rolled his. "I'd been here long enough to know that everything looks the same after a few days."

"All right." Kara stared at the spot. "That's where I'll focus the magic. Once Dario wakes up."

Chapter Seven

A FOOT SCUFFED nearby and she lifted her head from where she sat slumped against the wall.

"Kara."

She looked up to see Dario Todaro staring down at her. He set the second mage light down on the ground and sat down beside her.

"I remember everything," he said. "Thank you."

"You might not be grateful if we can't get out of here," she said.

"A simple 'you're welcome' is the appropriate response," he replied. "If it's going to happen, I'd rather die with my memories intact."

"Of course." She felt her cheeks heat with embarrassment. "I didn't mean . . ." She stopped, because that was exactly what she'd meant—that being mad—*dying* mad—was better than dying sane. "Sorry, your madness was a curse—a form of punishment. Of course, you'd rather be sane if . . ." she trailed off, not wanting to put their possible fate into words.

"Let's hope none of us dies," Dario said. "How is it you think I can help?"

Kara met his eyes and smiled. "My mother was lucky to have you as a friend." *And didn't deserve you*, she thought. Instead she got to her feet and held out her hand for him to take.

"I will need you to try to create spells or at the very least collect magic that I will direct."

"I CAN ALWAYS create mage lights," Dario said. "It's what has always given me—and others—hope that one day I could do real magic."

"But mage lights are real magic," Kara said.

They were leaning against one wall staring across at the one they wanted—needed—to tunnel through. Chal—he'd finally found out the Seyoyan's name—had gone to the spring to see if he could somehow collect a few drops of water.

And both Kara and Chal, to his astonishment, could see magic—could see spells!

Even in the workroom, he'd heard rumours that such people existed, but he'd never fully believed it. Just as he'd never fully believed in Assassins. Yet apparently one was on the other side of this cave wall trying to dig them out. Or he had been until they'd heard the cave-in.

He could tell that Kara was afraid—Chal was too, but at times Kara's fear and worry seemed to come off her in waves—that this Assassin had been caught in the cave-in.

"Mage lights are magic," he agreed. "But it's the simplest spell—one of the very first children are taught—so it's not much."

"You're pale blue," Kara said.

"What?" He was confused. "Pale blue? What does that mean?"

"The colour of your magic," she said. "Your mage mist. It's a pale blue colour. Like the sky."

"Oh, interesting." To be honest, since childhood, he hadn't actually seen the sky very often. He'd spent most of his days in the workrooms—arriving when it was dark and leaving when it was dark. "Is that an unusual colour?"

"Not really. All Mages have their own colour," she said. "That's how I know Valerio Valendi cursed you. He also cursed Santos."

"Santos. Do you mean Santos Nimali?" He only knew of one Santos—a few years ago he'd been the Mage Guild Primus. He'd visited the workroom once, although Dario hadn't spoken to him.

"Yes, I helped him the same way I helped you," she said matter-of-factly, as though she dealt with the most powerful Mages daily. And maybe she did?

"He has an estate on Old Rillidi," Kara continued. "That's where I live. He'll welcome you, if you want to joins us."

"I . . ." What did one say to that? "I'll certainly consider it, but we need to get out of here first." And he was starting to think that they might actually do it—that Kara might actually be able to do what she was planning on doing: taking his power and using it to tunnel through rock.

"All right," she said. "I need you to collect all the magic you can."

He tried to concentrate on drawing power to him, on feeling it fill him up with energy, but after a few moments of nothing, he shook his head.

"I'm sorry."

"Why did you stop?" Kara asked.

"I didn't think it was working. Was it?"

"Yes. The mage mist is so thick I can barely see your hands. You can't feel it?"

"No, I didn't think it was working." He'd been told by everyone that he would *feel* the energy when he was collecting magic. Had they been wrong all this time? "Do you think I can do spells by myself?"

"Do you want to try?" Kara stood up and held out her hand. He grabbed it, and she helped him to his feet.

"Other than lights I've never been able to create spells," he said. "So they stopped telling me how to do it. Do you know?"

"I think it's about intent," Kara said. "You need to think about what you intend to happen, then . . . I don't know, throw the magic at it? What do you do when you create a mage light?"

"I think about the need for a light." He smiled. He could do this. "Ready?" She nodded, and he focused on the wall in front of him; on making a passageway that would lead them outside. Then he tried to throw his magic at it.

"Get down!" Kara slammed into him just as air rushed past him and something smashed into the rock behind him. Dust and rock showered down on them.

"Did it work?" Chal burst into view and stopped. "Are you two all right?"

Dario gently rolled over; Kara was still partially wedged against him. He brushed dust off of them both and gingerly got to his feet. Chal bent down and helped Kara up.

"I think I need more practice," he said. Then he grinned. "But I did it—I actually created a spell that blasted the rock!" He was a Mage—after all these years—he was truly a Mage.

"Next time I'll be prepared to direct the spell," Kara said and smiled back at him.

Suddenly he heard the sound of something hammering on rock.

"What—?"

"Shhh," Kara said. "Be quiet." She and Chal both rushed to the opposite wall and pressed their ears to it.

The banging came again, in a pattern that could only be manmade. Chal smiled and stepped back, searching the ground. He picked up a rock and pounded on the wall with it, then sat waiting, his ear pressed to the wall.

KARA HELD HER breath; was it Reo? Would there be a reply to Chal's message, proving that Reo was alive?

She waited, not daring to breathe, not wanting to make a sound. There! Was that a reply? She stared at Chal. When a grin split his face, she closed her eyes as relief and happiness coursed through her.

"It's Reo," Chal said; he held up a hand as the tapping sounds continued. After a few moments, he stepped back from the wall, still smiling.

"They had a few injuries," he said. "Some bruises and one black eye, but nothing worse. It's taken them this long to clear out the debris and make sure the ceiling won't collapse again. Reo was very relieved to find out that we're alive." He paused. "What do you want me to tell him to do? Should they continue?"

"Tell them to stand back and let us try to get out with magic," Kara said. She looked over at Dario. "As long as you're comfortable with that?"

"Yes, I think we can do it."

She leaned in closer to Chal. "Tell Reo that if we're not through the rock in a few hours we'll need to rely on them to get us out."

"All right." He hammered out his message, pausing every few moments to listen to a reply.

"That's done," Chal said, stepping away from the wall. "Let's hope this works: we have very little water left." He held up the waterskin. "I was able to add a few drops from the spring but that's all there is, so be careful with it."

"All right." Kara didn't take the waterskin; she'd wait until she and Dario had a chance to try to use magic to make a way out; until she knew just how desperate their situation was.

She turned to the Mage. Mage mist wrapped round his balled fists. "You've already been collecting magic. Are you ready to try again?"

"Yes."

Chal edged out of the way as Dario stepped up to the wall. He held his hands up, palms facing the wall.

"I'll try to push it towards that wall," he said.

"I'll help." Kara steeled herself for the force of magic as a cloud of mage mist flowed from Dario's hands. But instead of hitting the wall and burrowing into it, it careened off it and slid along the ceiling.

"Down!" Kara said, but Chal was already dragging Dario to the ground. She reached up and shoved both hands into the mage mist, willing it to come to her, to respond to her demand. Slowly the mage mist started twining around her hands until all of the magic was spinning faster and faster above her head.

The magic sparked and flashed as it continued to collapse into a tighter and tighter ring around her hands. Slowly she lowered her arms and pointed the mist at the wall in front of her. With a mental heave, she thrust the mage mist towards the wall, willing it to dig into the earth.

There was a loud crack when the magic hit the wall. For a moment, the rock face seemed to buckle, and then the mage mist, still spinning, bit into it. Rocks and dirt were flung outward as the magic—it wasn't a spell, exactly—continued to burrow into the wall, filling the cave with the sound of rock being torn apart.

Kara shielded her eyes to try to watch what was happening. There was now a hole in the wall and she could see wisps of mage mist streaming from it. But it wasn't very big: just the diameter of the mage mist that had wrapped around her hands and not large enough for any of them to crawl through.

"Dario!" she called over the noise. "Gather more magic and come here!"

The Mage, dodging the rocks and dirt that were still spewing from the hole in the wall, staggered over to her. He lifted his hands: they were blanketed in mage mist and she gripped them.

"Think of a spell," she said to him. "But don't try to cast it."

When Dario nodded that he was ready, Kara *pulled* the magic from him. When all of the power had transferred from his hands to hers, she stepped up to the wall.

With each hand about a foot on either side of the hole, she pushed against the wall, willing the magic into it.

And was blown back by a burst of energy. She slammed into Dario, who cushioned her as they were pushed into the wall behind them.

Dazed, she looked at the wall; the hole was wider—wide enough for them to crawl through, she hoped. Drained, she slumped down and covered her ears with her hands to wait until the magic had finished . . . doing what it was doing. Even if the opening wasn't large enough to use to escape, right now she didn't have the energy to do anything more.

WHEN THE SPELL stopped—or broke through or dissipated—the cavern went silent. Kara lifted her head off her chest. Had the magic run out of energy? Had it been blocked by something more solid than rock? Or had it broken through to where Reo and the sailors were and . . . ?

She scrambled to her feet and over to the wall. It hadn't been a spell: it hadn't had any real direction, other than when she'd pointed it at the wall. Had it burst through to Reo and the others and caught them all by surprise? Had they survived the cave-in only to be killed by runaway magic? By the magic she'd sent their way?

"Reo!" she yelled into the ragged tunnel. "Reo! Are you there? Are you all right?" she called when what she meant was *were you alive*.

There was no answer. She was about to crawl into the hole when Chal's hand on her arm stopped her.

"We told them to stand back," he said. "And they would have heard the sound of the magic tunnelling through rock. I doubt they were close."

She met his eyes. He seemed so confident that she felt her panic drain away. "But what if they were too close?" she asked.

"They had Javan Losi," Chal said. "He would have seen the magic and gotten them all out of the way."

"Yes, you're right." Javan would have seen the magic. Her shoulders relaxed, and she took a step back to stand beside Dario, who was staring at the hole in the wall with a look of wonder on his face.

DARIO DIDN'T WANT to look away. He'd done magic; real magic, not simple mage lights. It hadn't precisely been a spell, and he hadn't directed it—but his power—his magic—had fuelled whatever Kara had done to drill through the rock wall. It was actually quite similar to the workroom, except there he never saw his power working: it was drained from him for use somewhere else. It was very different seeing how strong his magic was and what it could do.

And after a lifetime of feeling like a failure—of *being* a failure—he finally felt as though he'd lived up to his potential. If he never did anything magically significant again in his life, he would always have this moment, this feeling of *success*.

"What was that?" He dragged his gaze away from the wall to focus on Chal.

"Can you create a new mage light?" Chal asked. "And send it into the tunnel?"

"Yes, of course." He tried not to grin at this simple request, but he was needed—his magic was needed—again. He created a small mage light and had it float just outside the entrance to the narrow tunnel. "Do you want it to go inside?"

"Let me get in first," Chal said. "I'll try to see if everything looks stable or if I think it's collapsing."

He climbed into the hole. It wasn't wide enough for him to turn around but when Dario heard the other man's muffled "*now*" he pushed the mage light into the opening. It sped across the Seyoyan's shoulder and was lost to his sight.

"Do you want another one?" Dario asked. After being so proud of his magic, he was feeling a little deflated. He could create as many mage lights as they needed; what he couldn't do was control them.

"Can you slow it down?" Kara asked him.

"I'll try." He created another mage light and let it hover overhead. Concentrating on making it move slowly, he herded it into the hole. It too sped past Chal and down the tunnel.

The Seyoyan backed out of the tunnel. By the time he was standing, he was covered in dust.

"From what I could see the tunnel seems sound," he said. "And very straight. I think it's safe to travel."

"I'll go first," Kara said. "In case the magic got stuck in it somehow."

"No," Chal said. Then he sighed. "Yes, it's the only thing that makes sense. But you won't be able to let us know if anything's happened to you."

"Neither would you," Dario said. He wondered if they expected him to go first: he'd be able to send a mage light back, but he wouldn't be able to see any magic. And he certainly couldn't do anything about any magic that he might encounter. "I can create another mage light that you can take with you."

Kara slid her head into the opening and pushed with her legs until she was completely inside. Rather than have her try to carry or push a mage light ahead of her, Dario had fixed one to her shoulder right beside her ear. The light it cast illuminated the path ahead, except for the shadow of her head.

"I'll have Reo message you," she called over her shoulder, squinting at the glare of the light. Then she started forward, wriggling on her stomach and using her elbows to inch herself through the tunnel.

As Chal had said, the tunnel was straight. She could see a light at the other end but the tunnel was far longer than she'd expected. Men with pickaxes would have taken days—maybe weeks—to dig through all this rock.

"Hello?" Kara called. "Hello!" The light ahead of her flickered and grew stronger—a flame then, not a mage light—and she hurried towards it.

"Kara?"

"Reo." She crawled another foot and then hands gripped her and she was pulled from the tunnel and into his arms.

"I was so worried," she said as she collapsed against him. She sighed and looked over his shoulder. Torchlight cast shadows on half a dozen men who stood in a circle, staring at her.

"I take it you found the Mage responsible for all the magic on the island."

Kara turned her head to see Javan Losi, hands on his hips, staring at her. Self-consciously she stepped out of Reo's embrace.

"Yes," she agreed. "A Mage by the name of Dario Todaro." She looked back at Reo. "He was cursed by Valerio Valendi."

"Valendi." Reo scowled. "Still causing harm even after his

death. And Chal is well? He didn't say, and I worried that it was because he didn't want to alarm us."

"Yes," Kara said. "He's in good health. We all are. I told Chal we'd signal once I made it out safely."

"I'll do that now," Reo said. He picked up a heavy-looking hammer and headed to one side of the tunnel opening. He hammered on the rock.

"I saw the mage mist as it came through," Javan said, pulling her attention away from Reo. "Although we heard it before it got this far."

"Chal said that you'd be here," Kara said. "And that you'd make sure the magic didn't hurt anyone. I . . ." she paused, "I didn't have any way of making it stop once it dug through the rock, and I was worried that someone on this side would get hurt."

"It was certainly strange," Javan said. "Two separate spells broke through. Once free of the rock they stopped spinning so fast. Most spells dissipate when they've done what they were created to do but these seemed to almost merge together before settling on the ground and twisting out towards the mouth of the cave. I ran after them, but they were gone by the time I made it outside."

"They weren't spells," Kara said.

Reo rejoined them. "Chal and the Mage are on their way," he said. "What wasn't a spell?"

"The magic that tunnelled through the rock," Kara said. "Dario has magic but the only actual spell he can do is to create mage lights. I used his power to create the way out."

"You did magic?" Reo asked.

"No, I—" Kara started and then stopped. How to explain what had happened? "I took his power—his magic—and aimed it at the cave wall. It works a little bit like how I deflect spells: except this was unfocussed power that somehow I made dig through the rock. And I drew the magic out of him. Chal calls what I do unmagic."

"Unmagic—that's new," Reo said. "Ah, there's Chal now."

As soon as Chal had been pulled from the tunnel, Dario's head poked out of it.

DARIO SQUINTED AS he was pulled out into the torchlight.

"Dario Todaro," Kara said. "This is Reo Medina and Javan Losi." She gestured to two men: a Tregellan and a Seyoyan.

"Thank you," Dario said to them. "For your help. I think I've been here for a while."

"Longer than me," Chal said. "By at least two weeks. That's when Javan saw the magic and sent for me."

"I'll do my best to clear all the magic away before we leave," Kara said. "There could still be dangerous spells on the island."

"Magic? Spells?" He'd done things to the whole island and not just the cave? "I hope I haven't ruined anything on this island while I was . . ." How to explain that he'd been cursed? And how had he done magic?

"I told them you had been cursed," Kara said. "I know you didn't mean to cause any harm."

"But I did?"

"No one lives here," Chal said. "So there shouldn't be any real consequences. And Kara said she'd take care of it."

"Of course." Kara Fonti, who had somehow used his magic to get them out of the cave, would remove any spells he'd created while he'd been mad. She was standing beside the man she'd introduced as Reo, looking at him the way he probably looked at her mother. And despite that, something about Reo made him shiver; the man felt dangerous.

"I've had enough of caves," Chal said. "I hope it's a sunny day." He eyed him. "You coming outside, Dario?"

Chal headed off down a rocky trail, and Dario hurried to catch up to him.

"We didn't have a chance to talk about how you came to be in the cave with me," Dario said. They rounded a corner, and a gust of wind plucked at his hair. Up ahead the mouth of the cave was outlined in bright light. He shielded his eyes against the glare.

"Javan also sees magic," Chal said. "He noticed magic—your magic—on this island and I was sent to investigate." Chal stopped just inside the entrance. "I followed the mage mist into the cave and then . . . I was stuck inside with you." He stepped out into sunlight and, eyes closed, lifted his face skyward.

Dario hesitated before he too stepped into the sun. It was warm on his skin and he took another deep breath. "There were always rumours about people who see magic, and now I know they were true. I've met three of you."

"Two who see it and one who can do so much more," Chal said. "But don't tell Mage Guild."

"I would never do that," Dario replied. "And what about Reo Medina? Does he see magic too?"

"Reo?" Chal laughed. "See magic? No, he's an Assassin—or was—my guess is that he's here in case the threat was non-magical." Chal shrugged. "And I doubt he wanted Kara to deal with this problem alone."

"I did notice that he seems to be important to Kara." Kara Fonti, who was remarkable and possessed extraordinarily dangerous abilities. Maybe it was a good thing that she knew an Assassin. Mage Guild would not like someone with her talents; not unless they could control her. And if she was an asset to some, she would be a threat to others: someone would try to kill her, eventually.

"It's nice to be outside," Kara said from behind him. "Isn't it?"

"You can't go back," Dario said to her. "You can't let Mage Guild have you." Even his love—Arabella Fonti—would want to either use Kara or harm her, though she was her daughter.

"Mage Guild is not going to hurt me," Kara said. "Not that they haven't tried."

"Kara's not an easy target," Chal said. "She killed Valerio Valendi and is still standing."

"Chal, you know that was self-defence," Kara said. "I didn't want to—didn't *mean* to—kill him."

"But you did?" Dario tried to keep the fear from his voice but from the look Kara sent he knew he'd failed. Kara had said that Valerio Valendi was dead, not that *she* was the one who had killed him. "Everyone said that he was the most powerful Mage in all of Mage Guild." And Arabella's lover; and according to Kara, the Mage who had cursed him.

"Come on," Kara said, stepping onto the path in front of them. "I desperately need to clean up and eat a hot meal."

"I didn't mean to offend her," Dario said to Chal, who shrugged.

"It's the truth," the Seyoyan said. "So I doubt she was offended." He turned and followed Kara along the trail.

Dario stared at their retreating backs. He was out of the cave and no longer cursed but what was he supposed to do? More slowly than the others, he started along the path. Valerio Valendi might be dead, but that didn't mean he could safely return to Mage Guild. Or that he wanted to. But he had nowhere else to go.

Chapter Eight

As she walked, Kara automatically dispersed any mage mist that remained near the trail. The light blue mist was what she'd followed to the cave—into the cave. She heard Chal's footsteps behind her but neither of them spoke.

She paused at a tree: mage mist twined around the trunk and the leaves looked like feathers. In moments, palm fronds waved in the gentle breeze.

"You don't have to do it all at once," Chal said, breaking their silence.

"I don't want to have to come back," she replied. "I just want to get to the ship and stay there." She shrugged. "I've had enough of caves."

"Me too," Chal agreed. "I much prefer the open skies."

Kara headed off the path, her arms waving as she dissolved mage mist. Chal followed her as she made her way to the top of the cliff she'd seen from the dory. Tentatively, she started to draw all of the mage mist to her. Slowly at first but eventually thick rivers of mage mist streamed to her.

Chal stepped away from the edge of the swirling mass but Kara reached out to it. Waving her arms, she concentrated on dispersing the magic.

"Very impressive," Chal said when the magic was gone.

Kara shrugged. "I'm just glad I figured out how to remove it without having to travel every foot of this island. I'm tired, though." She turned and headed back to the path, and Chal followed her back down to the beach.

Chal's dory was still overturned and the *Mizar* was anchored in the bay, although a second dory had been pulled up on the beach. Chal grabbed her hand and, with a laugh, pulled her knee deep into the surf.

"Hey!" Kara said. "That's cold!" But she didn't retreat even when a swell reached her waist.

"It's refreshing," Chal said. He ducked under the water and came up spluttering. When he shook his head, his braids swung wildly and drops of water sprayed her.

Laughing, Kara dove into the next wave. It *was* refreshing. She could feel the worry wash away along with the grime of the cave and the grit of crawling through the tunnel. She hadn't felt afraid—hadn't allowed herself to feel fear, or worry or despair, not while she was stuck and needed to concentrate on getting out. But now that it was over, she felt giddy.

By the time she came up for air, the current had carried her far enough away from the beach that she could no longer touch the bottom. She kicked her feet and feathered her arms, trying to stay at the surface. Her chin dipped under water and she leaned her head back in order to take a breath. Keeping her head above water was getting harder. The cold was seeping into her limbs, making her legs feel heavy—too heavy to move. Panicky, she knew she should call for help but it took all of her energy—all of her breath—to try to stay afloat. Her ears were under water and now her arms were starting to falter.

And then Reo was there. He pulled her back against his chest and lay flat, keeping her head above water. She sucked in a deep, shaky breath.

"Relax," he said into her ear. "I've got you."

And she did relax. She rested against him and pulled her feet up and out of his way, the same as she had when they'd jumped off Mage Guild Island. He towed them for a minute or so before he stood up, drawing her with him up onto the beach.

"Sorry," she said. "I didn't realize . . ." Then a blanket was tucked around her, and Reo helped her sit down in the sun, with her back against the overturned boat. "I'll get you something hot to drink." And then he was gone. She was aware of people moving around, aware that orders were being shouted, but she was too busy shivering to worry about it.

DARIO TOOK A step back at the fury in the Assassin's eyes as he shouted at three Seyoyans to get a fire going.

A bedraggled Kara sat shivering by an upside-down boat as the Seyoyans scrambled around the beach, picking up driftwood and then piling it at a fire pit.

Chal, wet from the sea, stood looking a little lost, then nervous as the Assassin descended on him.

"You almost let her drown," the Assassin said to the Seyoyan. "After she got you out of that Gyda forsaken cave, you almost let her drown." The Assassin paused to rub a hand across his eyes. "She can't swim. She *would* have drowned if I hadn't been here!"

And he was right. Dario had arrived on the beach just as Kara had dived into the waves. But he hadn't noticed anything wrong when she surfaced. Chal had been a few feet from her and he hadn't reacted, so Dario didn't think Kara had called for help.

Then he'd heard someone swear and the Assassin had raced past him, diving straight toward Kara. It wasn't until the Assassin reached her that Dario understood that she'd been struggling to keep her head above water—had in fact been drowning.

"I didn't realize she was in trouble," Chal said. "I . . . she didn't make a sound. I was right there and she didn't make a sound."

"They usually don't," the Assassin said. "Drowning is a quiet way to die."

Dario shivered. *An Assassin would know the quiet ways to die*, he thought. That's how he'd known Kara was in trouble; he'd watched someone drown before. Had he caused it?

The Assassin's initial anger seemed spent but Dario sensed the smouldering fury that he was keeping in check. The fire was burning and someone had put a pot on to heat. The Assassin poured the liquid into a mug and took it over to Kara. He sat down and pulled her against him and helped her sip from the mug.

Chal stood by the fire and Dario joined him.

"I didn't notice anything wrong either," he said to the Seyoyan. It wasn't an excuse—he wanted the other man to know that he too would have been responsible if the worst had happened.

"He'll never trust me again," Chal said. "At least not with her."

He sighed. "And I have something to tell him that he will not want to hear. It's not his decision—not mine either—but he'll blame me for it anyway."

"He loves her," Dario said, not wanting to think what an Assassin might do to the people who allowed his love to drown.

"Yes," Chal agreed. "Though he feels he doesn't deserve her so tries not to allow himself to." He sighed again.

Dario was handed a mug of tea and some hard bread and cheese. They would be setting out for the ship as soon as Kara was recovered, he was told, understanding that they meant as soon as the Assassin decided she was ready to travel.

He found a place in the sun—alone—and sipped the warm liquid and ate his food.

Chal was still by the fire—he too had a mug and some food— and the Assassin remained by Kara's side.

The rest of the party, after some huddled conversations with Chal, scattered around the small beach to wait.

Dario found it fascinating that the Assassin—a non-Seyoyan— seemed to be the one in charge. Until he realized that it wasn't so much in deference for him as it was concern for Kara. Not one of the men here wanted to do anything to risk her health or do anything that might cause her harm.

Javan strolled over to the Assassin and Kara; they were too far way for Dario to hear what they were saying but the Assassin rose, gently pulling Kara with him, and the sailors started breaking camp.

Dario joined Chal, who was kicking sand onto the fire.

"So, we're leaving?" he asked. "And going where?" No one had asked him where he wanted to go—not that he thought returning to Mage Guild was safe for him. Not that he ever again wanted to see the inside of a workroom.

"We're off to Yeend," Chal said. "Do you know it?"

"It's the capital of Seyoya, isn't it?" He'd heard the name a long time ago when everyone thought he'd have a useful talent and would need to know about the world.

"Yes. And the largest city. It covers most of the island. Oh, Reo," Chal called.

The Assassin turned, and Dario fought the urge to step away from Chal. The man did not look like he was in the mood for light chatter.

"I need to tell you something," Chal continued. "Before . . . well, before Kara mentions it."

Reo took a step until he was facing Chal, and now Dario did ease away. He wasn't sure how Chal could face the fury and anger in the other man's eyes.

"What about Kara?" the Assassin asked softly.

"She, uh, she was asking me about living in Seyoya," Chal said. "Whether I thought she could earn a living teaching about the guilds and helping Seyoyans learn Tregellan. I just thought you should know."

"Now I know."

"And I didn't want you to blame me for not telling you," Chal said quietly, but the Assassin had already walked away.

KARA DIDN'T PROTEST as she was bundled into blankets and Reo picked her up and handed her over the gunwale of the dory. A Seyoyan helped her settle into the seat, and then Reo jumped into the boat and sat beside her.

Once at the ship Reo helped her climb aboard. She was almost asleep by the time she was deposited on her bunk by him. She saw Sif Shadae behind Reo looking worried. She was helped out of her damp clothes, and when she stretched out, more blankets were layered on top of her.

WHY WAS SHE so tired? Kara lifted a hand to brush her hair out of her eyes and her hand got snarled in the still damp tangle of her hair. She'd been in the water with Chal and then . . . she remembered not being able to keep her head above water and being cold and so, so tired.

Then Reo had saved her. Of course, it was Reo. It was always Reo.

The bunk was swaying: was the ship moving? Were they heading for Seyoya? She sat up and pushed the blankets off. She was only wearing her small clothes, and they were still a little damp, so she hadn't been asleep very long.

She hopped out of bed and grabbed her pack. She pulled out a pair of trousers, a shirt, a fresh set of smallclothes, and some thick socks. The socks might not help her navigate the deck of the *Mizar* while it was under sail, but she was still chilled from being in the water.

Once dressed, she opened the door. The narrow hallway was quiet; a few lamps lit the way, swinging gently on hooks. She took the short set of stairs up to the galley.

The galley was empty at this time of night but it was ready for breakfast. She hadn't had enough to eat or drink in days and now, after almost drowning, she was hungry and thirsty.

She poured some water into a mug. It took her three mugs before she'd drunk her fill, and she turned her attention to food. A bundle that sat beside a crock of butter—once unwrapped—turned out to be journey bread.

She had just finished slathering butter on a second piece of bread when the door opened. A familiar head of white blond braids poked in.

"Chal! Are you hungry too?"

"Yes." Chal sat down, but he didn't reach for the bread. Instead, he put his hands on the table, palms up. "I'm sorry. I almost cost you your life."

"What?" Kara almost dropped the pieced of bread she held. "You did not. That was my fault. I'm the one who can't swim. And I didn't tell you."

"You could have died," he said. "Because I wasn't paying attention."

"You weren't," Kara agreed. "But who said you had to? Who made you my keeper?" She could guess. "Reo blames you." Chal nodded.

"He shouldn't," she continued. "Nor should you blame yourself." She eyed him. "Unless you think I'm not capable of making my own decisions? Or my own mistakes?"

"That's a trick question," Chal said, but he seemed to have relaxed.

"Of course, it is. You can't be responsible for me and my mistakes unless you take away my independence." She raised her slice of bread. "Which I will not allow." She shoved the rest of the bread into her mouth and chewed while Chal stared at his hands.

"I'm not sure Reo will see it that way," he said finally.

"Yes, I know," Kara said. "I can't make any promises, but I'll try to make him see that he's wrong." She pushed the half-loaf of bread towards him. "Have something to eat. And tell me where this ship is headed."

It was late by the time she returned to her cabin. She paused outside the door to Reo's cabin: she needed to talk to him about his treatment of Chal, but not tonight.

She entered her cabin and sat down on her bunk. She wasn't sure she'd be able to sleep, not after sleeping most of the day and night. Besides, she was excited. Yeend! They were going to Yeend, the capital of Seyoya. She wasn't sure how long they'd be there—just until they could get a ship back to Tregella she supposed—but surely there would be some time to explore the city.

And who would be going home? She and Reo, of course, but would Dario Todaro want to leave or would he decide to stay in Seyoya? She'd need to ask him in the morning. After she'd spoken to Reo about what had happened on the beach.

She'd thank him, of course, for saving her life. And then she'd make sure he didn't blame Chal.

She lay down, expecting to stare at the ceiling until dawn came.

Instead, she woke up to the bed swaying violently. She managed to get her feet on the floor without falling, but then the ship rolled and her sock-covered feet slid out from under her. Gripping the bunk, she lowered herself to the floor. She pulled her socks off before she stood up again. The room was small enough that she could reach the door with one hand still on the swinging bunk.

She yanked the door open and stepped out into the passageway.

There was no answer when she pounded on Reo's door—no answer from any of the doors she knocked on along the hallway. She stared at the end of the passageway and the stairs that led up to the deck, where everyone else must be.

Now she understood the presence of the rope railing that lined every single wall on the ship. She clung to it as she passed wildly swinging lamps and climbed the stairs to the next level.

She stood in the doorway to the galley. Far from the calm setting she'd shared with Chal last night, it was busy—but not with meal preparations. The cook—a burly sailor who was missing three fingers on one hand—shooed her away, explaining in Seyoyan that he was tying everything down.

She made her way up the second set of stairs to the deck. Wind whipped at the sails as men scrambled among them. Captain Arends was on an upper deck, shouting orders. The sky was angry, and dark clouds roiled above the shuddering sails.

It was dry, but Kara thought the rain would hit at any minute. And despite their southern destination and its warmer climate, it was cold. A wave hit, and the ship rolled as seawater sprayed over the gunwales.

Someone gripped her arm from behind, and she looked back and met Reo's eyes.

"You should be downstairs," he said. "Come on." He steered her towards the stairs she'd just emerged from, following her to the second landing.

"There's a cabin," he said. "Where we can wait it out."

He led the way along the corridor, and she hurried after him. She was damp from the spray and her feet were cold, and she would be no help on deck.

THE DOOR OPENED, and the Assassin—Dario had a hard time calling such an intimidating man by his name—entered, followed by Kara.

"Kara, come join us." He ignored the Assassin's glare and helped her to a seat. He pulled the blanket off his chair and handed it to her. "I think they want us all out of the way." He sat back down. The Assassin narrowed his eyes, but he pretended to not see it. He was not giving up his chair—next to Kara—for Reo Medina.

"I looked in on you earlier," Chal said. "But you were sleeping. I didn't want to wake you if you could sleep through the whole thing."

"Was the captain expecting bad weather?" Kara asked.

"No." The Assassin made his way to the other side of the table—a feat Dario was in awe of considering the ship was pitching and rolling violently—and sat across from Kara. "He said it was very unusual for this time of year."

"Unusual," Kara repeated softly, and Dario stared at her. What did that mean? Did she think someone from Mage Guild had sent a storm their way?

The wooden ship creaked and groaned as the angry sea tossed it; every few moments a wave crashed against the nearby hull. The wind must have snatched away any voices because Dario couldn't hear any shouts from on deck. The four of them seemed to be the only ones on the ship not actively sailing it.

"Have you been to Seyoya before, Kara?" he asked, partly because he wanted a distraction from the storm.

"No," she replied. "I'm looking forward to it though. And you, are you planning on staying or will you return to Rillidi?"

"I . . ." He didn't have an answer. "I'm not sure it's safe for me to go back to Rillidi." He had been cursed by the Mage Guild Secundus, who was now dead, but that didn't mean he would be safe. "But can I truly leave Mage Guild?" He'd been reconciled with a life outside of Mage Guild when he was told he was being exiled but that had been a punishment. Could he hope for something better?

Kara reached over and patted his hand. "You'll be unguilded, like me." She looked at Reo. "And Reo, and all of us on Old Rillidi. You could join us there if you wish."

"Or stay on Yeend," Chal said. "You can make mage lights and I'll help you sell them."

Dario looked at the Seyoyan to see if he was joking, but he didn't seem to be. "Is that something that would have value?" Mage lights were so simple that it took the most basic of talents. Which was why even he could create them.

"Yes," Chal said. The ship listed to one side, and they all hung onto the table until the ship rolled back straight.

"Take this ship," Chal continued. "It's filled with oil lamps. On a day like this, those lamps pose a danger. Every captain with enough funds would replace them with mage lights, if they could."

"Mage Guild won't like it," he said, but he was already grinning. "But it might be years before they know. And I would like more days in the sun." He could do it—he could make mage lights—he could always make mage lights. And even if Mage Guild realized that someone was creating them, would they really bother sending a Mage to investigate? He was actually starting to believe that he could really live a life free from the guilds.

"And what about Kara?" the Assassin said. "I heard that you plan on staying in Seyoya too."

KARA STARED AT Reo. "It had crossed my mind," she said. She looked over at Chal, who was staring at the table. This wasn't how she wanted to discuss any of this, but if Reo thought she would back down, he was mistaken. "I have a life I will return to, but I thought some time away might be good for me."

"I see," Reo said. He looked away, and she saw him swallow. "You should do what's best for you. I can tell Santos and the others."

She stared at him, aware of Dario and Chal watching and listening, but not caring. "Will you stop it?" she said. "Will you for once tell me what you want? Tell me I can't stay away because it would invalidate the contract with Warrior Guild. Tell me that would send you back to them and you'd hate being an Assassin again. Tell me what you want." *Tell me you want me,* she thought, *tell me you want me!*

"I . . ." Reo stopped and closed his eyes, and she hoped he would actually say something she wanted to hear.

"Kara Fonti!" someone called from outside. "Kara Fonti!" The door was flung open, and a soaked and dishevelled Javan Losi stood in the doorway. "You're needed on deck, right away. There's magic fuelling this storm, and Captain Arends thinks we're lost unless you can defeat it."

Chapter Nine

KARA LET HIM lead her to the deck: her fight with Reo would have to wait. She greeted Captain Arends and stared out into the storm, trying to see the magic, but all she saw was spinning clouds and . . . there! She pointed over the gunwale to a spinning mass of light blue. The mage mist was whipping the sea into angry, spiralling waves. One of the waves hit the ship, and seawater gushed across the deck, almost sweeping a sailor off his feet.

"That's it," Javan said over the sound of the wind. "We've tried to outrun it but it's following us. I think someone sent it after us."

"No." As Kara stared, the mage mist split into two, and one part spiralled up into the sky. She recognized that colour: knew whose magic it was. "It's the magic I used to tunnel out of the cave," she said. "The magic that wasn't a spell so it didn't stop when the task was completed." It was the magic that *she'd* unleashed on the world. She squared her shoulders. So it was up to her to use her talent—her *unmagic*—to stop it.

"I need to get closer," she said to Reo, who had followed her on deck. He nodded and turned to the captain.

Kara ignored their conversation. She trusted Reo to get her what she needed so that she could do what she had to do. What only she could do. She trusted Reo with her life, so she concentrated on the magic.

There were three separate fragments now, from what she could tell: the two original masses of magic, one of which had now somehow twinned.

She could see one out at sea, just to their left, and the other two were above the ship, in the wind. The two in the wind were smaller and weaker, so she decided to tackle them first.

"I need to be there." She turned to Reo and pointed to the main mast. She hoped that she could do this from the deck, but if she had to climb up the sails or be hauled up into the air—she'd do it.

"All right." Reo looped rope around both of their waists, cinching them together. The other end was tied to a railing, and sailors were slowly feeding the rope out to Reo.

Kara nodded, and with Reo tight against her back, she walked towards the mast. The wind buffeted her and the sea washed across her path a few times, but Reo's steady strength kept her upright.

Once she reached the main mast, she reached a hand out. The wood was wet beneath her hand: she craned her neck to look above her. A few sailors were clinging to the rigging, and above them, a spiral of mage mist whipped around the canvas sails.

"Hold on," she said over her shoulder to Reo. She reached up with both hands and willed the mage mist to come to her. Slowly, very slowly, the mist started to curl down towards her, spinning more tightly until it was a rope of pale blue mist.

She'd drawn the mage mist on the island to her with ease, but none of that had the power and intensity and *fury* of this magic. She continued to pull it to her until it spun tightly just above her raised hands. On tiptoe, she reached a hand into the magic. And was blown back into Reo. Somehow, he kept them both on their feet, and the magic, most of its energy now spent, slowed. Threads of gauzy mage mist wafted off the column and dissolved. After a few moments, the mage mist was gone.

The wind was noticeably calmer, and she sagged against Reo, who had wrapped his arms around her waist.

"Are you all right?" he asked in her ear. She nodded and took a deep breath. She was still tired from the ordeal in the cave and her near drowning, but she wasn't done, not yet. There were still two more masses of magic to deal with.

It started to rain, as though the mage mist she'd destroyed had been holding it back—and maybe it had been. Kara wiped her hair off her face, and with a hand shielding her eyes against the rain, tried to find the second mass of mage mist amongst the sails.

It was higher than the first had been but it came to her more easily, as if the energy of the first mass had been feeding into this one and keeping it aloft. She was more careful and took more time to drain the magic. Wisps of pale blue thinned and dissipated as they flowed towards her. By the time it was gone, she was soaked and shivering.

"Come on," Reo said. "You need a rest."

She would have protested but she didn't have the energy; so she gave in, since he was right. She did need a rest.

The wind still whipped at the sails but it was less intense than it had been. She spotted the pale blue mage mist in the sea, hoping that it too had weakened. Then Reo untied them and helped her get below deck.

THE DOOR OPENED, and Kara and the Assassin came back inside, wet and bedraggled. The Assassin helped Kara into a chair before leaving again. He returned a few minutes later with a couple of blankets.

"I'll fetch some tea," Chal said, leaving him alone with Kara and her Assassin.

He was afraid to speak, afraid to take the Assassin's attention from Kara. Afraid to even watch him, although he did, out of the corner of his eye.

The Assassin wrapped Kara in blankets, using one to gently dry her hair. Dario felt like he was intruding on something intimate, and he was grateful when Chal returned with a tray.

A few minutes were spent getting tea poured and handed out, but eventually that was done, and Chal sat down.

"I can watch her while you change," Chal said. "Then Kara should put on something dry."

"No," the Assassin said. "I'll stay."

"Reo," Kara said. "I'll be safe with Chal. You go change and bring me back something dry to wear."

"You weren't safe with him last time," the Assassin said, and Chal sucked in a breath.

Dario would have left if he could have gone unnoticed. As it was, he fixed his gaze on the cabin wall behind Chal so he didn't stare at anyone.

"I didn't have a chance to thank you," Kara said. "For saving me. From my own mistake."

"Chal would have let . . ." The Assassin stopped talking as though he couldn't bear to put his next thought into words.

"Maybe," Kara said gently. "So I am grateful to you. But Chal is not responsible for me. And neither are you. *I am.* Unless I ask you to be, like—" she waved a hand "—now, when I've asked you to change and fetch me some dry clothes." She tucked her hand under the blanket and shivered. "So, will you? Please? I need to go back out there. I'm not finished. And I need your help."

"All right." The Assassin stopped at the door to glare at Chal. "I'll be back very soon."

There was a brief moment of silence, then Chal spoke. "That went better than I expected it to." He poured another mug of tea and slid it across to Kara. "And what exactly are you not finished doing?"

"The magic," Kara said. She sighed, and Dario realized that she was exhausted. And that the fighting between the Assassin and Chal was draining even more of her energy. "I've dispersed some of it but there's still more out there." She looked across the table and met his eyes. "And Dario, it's *your* magic. Our way out of the cave has managed to create this storm."

"My magic." He was stunned. As a Mage he had always been a failure, and yet now his magic threatened them all. "Tell me what I can do to help." He'd been excited—and proud—that his magic had helped them all escape. But what if the ship foundered and sank? If Kara was lost—if she couldn't stop it—would his magic continue on a destructive path? Would it cross the sea, growing in strength until it threatened more ships and then eventually the islands of Seyoya? Disguised as a natural storm, his magic could destroy so much, hurt so many people. It had to be stopped.

"I'm not sure you *can* help," Kara said. "I'd be afraid to use your magic again."

"No, you're right." He didn't want to let more of his magic loose on the world either.

He looked up when the Assassin returned, but he was so worried about the destruction his magic might cause that he forgot to be afraid of him. "But maybe you can somehow, I don't know, put my magic back into me?"

"Can you do that?" the Assassin asked. He handed Kara some clothes and she stood up.

"Take a corner, each of you," she said to Chal and the Assassin, and they held a blanket while she changed. "I don't know," Kara said. "All of this is new, so maybe." She stepped out from behind the blanket wearing faded trousers and a dingy once-white shirt. "But I was able to get rid of two of the masses of magic. I should be able to get rid of the last one." She sat back down and picked up her tea.

"But there was only two," Dario said. "To begin with. You only used magic twice, didn't you?"

"Yes," Kara replied. "But I saw a smaller section split off from the main mass. That's why I need to get back out there. In case it divides again." She handed her mug to Chal and picked up the blanket. "I need to get back out there, Reo."

"All right," the Assassin said. "I'm coming with you."

"And me," Chal said. "I can help keep an eye on the mage mist."

"No," the Assassin said. He glared at Chal, who lifted his chin. "I can't trust you."

"Just Reo," Kara said softly. "Chal, please, I don't want to risk anyone else." Kara wrapped the blanket around her and headed to the door. She looked determined to battle the magic, but Dario could see that she was worried.

"Just me," the Assassin agreed, with another look at Chal. He opened the door for Kara. He was about to follow her when Dario—without planning what he was doing—reached a hand out to stop him.

Dario stood up and nervously looked into the Assassin's angry face.

"She needs your support," he said. "Not this bickering between you and Chal."

The Assassin closed the door and leaned over him. "Bickering? Is that what you think I'm doing?"

"It's not what you think you're doing," Dario said. "But it's what she's hearing. And feeling. She wouldn't like the comparison, but she's stubborn, like her mother." He sighed. "She's exhausted and has to do something only she can do. Help her."

"Why do you care, Mage?"

"That's my magic she's battling," he said. "I can't control it—I *never* could control it—and now it could kill us and maybe hundreds more if it's not stopped. I really don't want to have to live with knowing I'd caused so much destruction."

The Assassin looked at him for a long time before he nodded and left the room.

KARA STARED OUT at the storm. Reo arrived and handed her a coat made of oiled cloth, and she dropped the already damp blanket and shrugged into the coat.

"Should I have the *Mizar* head into her?" Captain Arends asked as he leaned close. "By my reckoning, the eye of this storm is just off our starboard side." He pointed over the right-hand railing. A huge mass of light blue mage mist roiled and twisted, causing waves to curl and crest in the sea.

"Try to stay beside it," Kara said. Had the mage mist gotten bigger? Was the storm—caused by magic—now powering the mass of wild magic? Had it somehow become something that fuelled—and was fuelled by—itself?

"Reo!" She'd made a mistake. She should have concentrated on the main mass and left the smaller two that she'd already destroyed for later. "Tie me in now!"

Reo stepped up behind her and wrapped the rope around both of them.

"Here we go," he said. "You worry about the magic, and I'll worry about keeping us on our feet."

She looked over her shoulder and met his solemn gaze. She nodded, grateful for his steady strength. She wouldn't be able to fight the wind and rolling deck *and* the magic. And she trusted him to keep them on her feet. She would need every ounce of energy and talent she had in order to win this battle.

She was aware of Reo's warmth at her back as she took a few steps closer to the railing and the storm. A wave washed over the railing, and the sea—knee deep—swept across the deck. She took another step, anchored by Reo, and then she was able to grip the wood with both hands.

Sparks flashed just above the waves. She reached one hand out and started to draw the magic to her, trying to extract a thin thread. A wisp of light blue started towards her but then the mass twisted and the wisp was drawn back into it.

"I need both hands," she said to Reo. She felt his arms tighten against her sides as his hands replaced hers on the railing.

With both hands free, she stretched them out to the mage mist, forcing it to respond. And it did, but not the way she'd hoped. A layer of mage mist suddenly broke free of the main mass. It started to twist in the wind, spiralling up into the sky, but she reached for it, forcing it down and away from the rest of the magic. It fought her, and she pushed at it, trying to keep it from re-joining the larger mass.

The sheet of mage mist raced over the railing and slammed into her, rocking her backwards into Reo. Then the mage mist vanished: contact with her—with whatever immunity she had against magic—had been more than it could survive.

And she suddenly knew what she had to do. She signalled Reo to take her back to the captain.

"You need to lower me into the storm," she said when she reached Captain Arends. "Do you have something that can do that?" Reo tensed, and she prepared for his argument.

"I'm going with you," was all he said. "You still need my help."

She blew out a breath. She did need his help. And if she was honest with herself, his solid presence gave her more than physical strength; it gave her the confidence to head into danger. And this would be very dangerous.

"I'll have the men set up a rig," Captain Arends said. "It'll just take a few minutes."

After untying them, Reo herded her inside to wait. Javan handed them mugs of hot tea but after that, they were left alone at the head of the stairs.

"They all think we might die," Kara said.

"People have thought that about us before," Reo said. "*We've* thought that about us before. But we survived jumping off Mage Guild Island while being chased by a powerful Mage. Being lowered into a magical storm seems almost tame in comparison."

She shook her head, grateful that he was at least pretending that they could do this and survive.

"Can I ask you a question?" Reo said quietly. "Since I may not have another chance?"

She nodded. "I might not answer." She heard his chuckle.

"I know that." He paused for a moment. "You finally have the home you wanted," he said. "So why are you really thinking about staying in Seyoya?"

She closed her eyes. She wouldn't lie to him, not about this, but she could choose not to answer. But if this was what he wanted to know before they went to their possible deaths, he deserved the truth.

"I'm trying to figure out how to live my life without you." It was actually easier to say than she'd thought it would be, maybe because she wasn't looking at his face.

"Why—"

The ship lurched, and Javan rushed in through the door, sea spray accompanying him.

"Whatever you're going to do, you need to do it now," Javan said. "Come on!"

Kara and Reo followed Javan out onto the deck. A winch had been moved out into the middle of the deck, and a sailor handed Javan a rope harness.

"Here, get into this, and we'll raise you up."

Kara and Reo stepped into the harness, pulling the straps up and over their shoulders. Javan tied half a dozen ropes, tightening them so that her back was pressed against Reo, but their arms were free. Reo wrapped his around her waist. She covered his hands with her own and nodded to Javan.

"Hoist them up!" he called. A couple of sailors started walking around the winch in a circle, pushing the wooden handles. The rope attached to the harness went taut and Kara felt her feet leave the deck.

Immediately the wind started twisting them, spinning them as the arm of the winch swung them closer to the side of the ship.

Javan grabbed the harness and steadied them as he accompanied them to the railing. Once they were high enough off the deck, Javan pushed them out over the water and let go.

Kara took a deep breath as they spun above the angry sea. A few feet to her right the mage mist—a thick cable of it—roiled and twisted.

And then they were being lowered into the maelstrom. Reo's arms tightened around her waist, and she knew she could do this—*would* do this—because she had to.

DARIO HADN'T BEEN able to stay below, but he hadn't wanted to watch, either, so he huddled at the rear of the deck, behind the

Captain and the wheel, where three sailors were trying to hold the ship steady against the battering wind and sea. And magic.

But he saw when Kara and her Assassin were sent over the railing, and he heard the order for the sailors manning the winch to start lowering it. And all he could think of was that it was his fault, that it was his magic that was causing such destruction. And there should be some way for him to help fix it.

He just didn't know what it was.

"This is a good spot to see all the action." Chal sat down beside him. "Ah, I see Reo is with her. Good."

"Yes," he agreed. "As long as he doesn't fight her." They were out of sight now, and Dario was tempted to find a spot near the railing and watch. But if it didn't work—if Kara and her Assassin were lost—he didn't want to witness it. "You saw it, didn't you? My magic."

"Yes," Chal said. "It is very powerful. I hope Kara can overcome it."

"No else could even try to," Dario replied. Which was why she had to survive this. Mage Guild had given him no choices—he could see that now—and they'd made his life small and dark. But Kara had the power to stand up to them. And even if it was her mother, the love of his life, who she was standing up to, someone had to.

Suddenly a wave crashed onto the deck, and two of the sailors manning the winch slipped and fell to their knees. The handles spun backwards a few turns before the sailors were able to recover and stop even more rope from unwinding.

THEY PLUNGED INTO the waves, and startled, Kara lost control of the magic. She cried out as the wind gusted and cold water reached her knees. Trussed together the way they were, she and Reo had no chance of keeping their heads above water if they dropped into the sea.

Their descent halted and the rope jerked tight. They dangled with their feet in water for a moment before they were pulled back above the waves.

The mage mist was still a few feet to her left. It was smaller now that she'd drawn some power from it but what was left was even more volatile.

Siphoning off some of the magic seemed to have destabilized

it, and now it spun and twisted erratically. A waterspout danced towards them, and she reached out to it, pulling at the magic that fed it. Its energy gone, the spout fell apart and dropped back into the sea.

She was tiring—trying to control this wild magic drained her energy and the cold seeped into her. Except at her back, where she was pressed against Reo's heat.

She tried to drag her arms up again; then she felt Reo's hands on her wrists, holding hers in the air. She concentrated on the magic in front of her, on drawing it towards them, slowly, but she was too tired to maintain control.

Mage mist surged towards them, most of it dissolving as soon as it reached her but some of it sped past them towards the ship.

"Oh no," Chal said. "It's coming right at us."

Dario rushed out on deck. He saw the Assassin—Reo—and Kara, spinning at the end of the winch line, and then something crashed into the railing. He threw himself at it, concentrating with all his might at drawing his magic back to him. He was slammed to the deck, and then he felt his whole body tingle.

"Don't touch me!" he yelled at Chal, who had followed him. "Don't touch me!" He raised one arm—he could see it! He could see his magic, and it *was* the blue of a summer sky. *How ironic,* he thought, *to have magic the colour of a sky I've so rarely seen.* Then he started to twitch as the magic hummed through him. Even when he closed his eyes, he could see the light of his power.

"Get me down," Kara called. "Get me down!" Mage mist coursed around Dario's still form, the energy crackling and sparking.

Chal hovered over him, but at the sound of her voice, he waved towards the captain, who bellowed an order. The sailors on the winch started turning the handles, bringing her and Reo over the deck.

"Are you all right?" Reo asked in her ear.

She nodded. "The magic is gone, the storm is gone, but some of it hit Dario. I think he absorbed it . . . almost."

Her feet touched the slippery wood of the deck and hands scrabbled at the wet ropes and finally she was out of the harness. Reo helped her to Dario's side, and she ran her hands along his arms, trying to rub away the thick layer of mage mist that flowed over him.

A spark flashed and she shut her eyes against it. Ignoring everything else, she concentrated on drawing magic away from him. When she dragged her eyes open, Dario was still covered in mage mist, although it was transparent now. She didn't relax until she saw Dario's chest rise and fall as he breathed.

She dropped her arms—she was too exhausted to do anything more—and felt herself being lifted into someone's arms. She looked up at Reo's worried face.

"Dario," she said. At least, she tried to speak.

"You need to rest," Reo said.

She tried to speak again but didn't have the energy. Reo turned around, and she faced Dario, Chal kneeling at his side. The Seyoyan glanced up at her. The last thing she saw was his grim nod.

Chapter Ten

SHE STRETCHED, ENJOYING the feel of soft sheets under her.

"You're awake."

Kara opened her eyes to a sun-filled room and a bed that was not swaying. A Seyoyan woman sat by her side, her bright yellow top accentuating her dark skin.

"Where am I?" Kara asked in Seyoyan.

"I speak Tregellan," the woman replied in that language. "We are in Seyoya: Yeend to be exact. And before you ask, yesterday you were brought in by the dangerous-looking man who has been waiting outside this door ever since. I was told you overexerted yourself, which caused you to collapse from exhaustion. You've been sound asleep for over eight hours." She picked up a mug from a bedside table. "Here, drink this."

"What is it?" She sat up and took the mug and sniffed, wrinkling her nose at the odour. "I don't recognize it." It didn't smell appetizing, which made her think it probably was medicine. Who would try to use a poison that smelled so vile?

"It's noni," the woman said. "To give you energy. I'll order some fish broth too."

Kara hesitated and the woman smiled.

"Here." She grabbed the mug and took a sip before handing it back to Kara. "To prove I mean no harm. And my name is Taba."

"I would use nettle," Kara said. "For energy." She took a sip.

The liquid tasted bad, but not as bad as it smelled.

"You know healing arts?"

"Non-magical ones, yes." Kara didn't think the woman was out to hurt her so she gulped the noni down. She set the empty mug on the side table.

"Non-magical," Taba repeated. "That is all I have ever known, although I have heard of magic being used to heal. I would very much like to see that. Is it as good as they say?"

"It can be," Kara replied, thinking about Pilo's scars and how Santos was healing them. "But convincing a Mage to bother healing anyone is a challenge."

"Is it? Do you not think healing one of the most honourable tasks to undertake? Seyoyans think so."

"I do too," Kara said. "But I'm not a Mage." She felt very sleepy. "Are you sure that drink was to give me energy?"

"You need more sleep, but I didn't give you anything to help you do that," Taba said. "I'll just go and ask for that soup."

"Kara."

She sighed and rolled onto her back.

"Kara."

She opened her eyes. "Reo."

"Taba said you were awake and that I could visit for a few minutes."

"I was awake," Kara said. "But I'm still very tired." She pulled a hand out from under the covers, and he took it and helped her sit up, but he didn't let go of her hand once her back was leaning against the wall. "The storm? It's gone?"

"Yes." His hand tightened on hers. "The storm is gone and the ship arrived safely in Yeend—along with everyone on board—thanks to you."

"My fault," she said. "The storm." If she hadn't sent that unfocussed magic through the cave wall there wouldn't have been a storm.

"Dario says it was his fault, since it was his magic."

"He's safe too?" She remembered something about . . . "The power from the storm hit him."

"He says his magic came back to him," Reo said. "And now he and Chal have their heads together. Some sort of business idea."

"Of course." She knew what it was—didn't she? But everyone was all right. "Sleep," she murmured, or at least she thought she said it out loud.

"THAT'S TOO BRIGHT," Chal said.

Dario wiped a sleeve across his forehead. The magic in him—the power—was hard to control. And he wasn't surprised, since his magic had so recently fuelled that terrible storm. Along with a lot more power than what he'd absorbed.

"I can't help it," he told Chal, his new business partner. "The power comes out no matter how I try to minimize it." The business venture—a Merchant venture—was still confusing to him, but Chal was confident that, if Dario created the mage lights, Seyoyans would be lining up to buy them.

"Will these last longer than normal?" Chal asked. "Or will they burn out faster?"

"I have no idea." Dario concentrated on his open palm and soon a mage light sat on it. He placed the mage light next to the others he'd created.

He was finally feeling normal: his hair was no longer sticking up and he didn't create a spark every time he touched something.

"I think my magic is calming down," he said to Chal. "Can you tell?"

Chal eyed him. "Maybe. Most of the time I spent with you was when you were cursed, and even you think that made your magic work differently. So, it probably *looked* different too."

"Chal."

Dario looked up to see the Assassin—Reo—in the doorway to the small workroom.

Dario had been stunned and lying on the deck of the *Mizar*, but he'd still been aware of the man's frantic efforts to get Kara to safety. Captain Arends had raised all sails and gotten them to Yeend as soon as he could. And as far as Dario knew, Reo had never once left Kara's side. Not until now.

"Kara's awake," Reo said. "I just thought you should know."

"Thank you," Chal said stiffly.

"And thank you for sending Taba." Reo paused and then nodded awkwardly before leaving.

"He still hasn't forgiven me," Chal said with sigh.

"He can't forgive himself," Dario said. "For Kara being in danger yet again." He felt a frisson of power run through him, and the hair on his forearm lifted. "Get ready, I need to make another light."

KARA SIPPED THE fish broth. It was delicious, if a little spicier than what she was used to.

"Thank you, Taba." She held out the bowl and Taba ladled more broth in it. "I should be on more solid foods next meal, don't you think?"

"Healers," Taba said, "make the worst patients. But yes." She smiled, taking any sting out of her words. "Something more solid for your next meal."

Kara finished the second bowl of broth and set the bowl on the tray. "I appreciate everything you're doing. It's just that . . ."

"You hate being ill," Taba finished. "Every healer I know is the same. There's always too much to do to waste time in bed. But that is exactly where you need to stay for the next day or so." She picked up the tray. "No matter that you think you know better." At the door, she paused. "I'm your healer and that is my order."

"Do I have a choice?" She wasn't sure where her clothes were, nor did she know where she was, other than somewhere in Yeend. But she was tired, and as soon as Taba was gone, Kara felt herself drifting off.

"KARA." SHE LOOKED up to see Reo again, standing by the bed. "Mistress Taba said I could visit."

"Only because you scare her," Kara said. She sat up and leaned her back against the wall. "She called you dangerous."

"I think I'm more afraid of her than she is of me," Reo said. He smiled, and Kara smiled back, happy to see him so relaxed.

"Thank you." She held out her hand and he took it. "I don't remember much after seeing the magic hit Dario, so you must have gotten me here. So, thank you."

"You'd just saved us all," Reo said. He dropped her hand and glanced away from her for a moment. "Now that we're safely in Seyoya, I need to make arrangements to return to Old Rillidi."

"Oh, I'm sure I'll be able to travel in a few days," Kara said. "As long as I get more bedrest, Taba will probably agree."

"That's if . . . I mean." Reo paused. "I wasn't sure if you wanted to return right now."

"Well, I would prefer to take a few days and explore Yeend because who knows when I might be out this way again?" She watched Reo, who was deliberately not looking at her. "But that's not what you meant, is it?"

"No." Reo didn't seem to know what to do with his hands. "I thought you wanted to stay here." He looked away from her before meeting her eyes. "And teach, but I want . . . *need* to know what you meant when you said you were trying to figure out how to live your life without me."

Kara sighed. Now it was her turn to look away. "I, of all people—with the mother I have—know I can't force someone to care about me—to love me." She looked up at him. "No matter how much I might want it, no matter how much I might . . ." She looked away again. "Love them. So, I thought learning to live with that pain might be easier if I didn't have to see them—see *you*—every day."

"I do love you," Reo said quietly, and her heart soared. "But I keep making decisions that end up taking away your choices. Decisions that put you in danger, like when I took you to your mother." His eyes dropped to the floor. "I don't want to do that to you."

"But don't you see?" Kara asked. "I won't allow you to take away my choices—I *didn't* allow it. You took me to see my mother because you were angry that you *could not force me* to do what you wanted me do."

"And we almost died," Reo said. "Because of my angry decision."

"But we didn't." She sighed. "Remember what you said about *why* you took me to see my mother, the woman who wanted me dead? You said you wanted someone to fight for you the way I fight for the ones I love. I need that from you too. And it's not just about saving me, about making sure I stay alive, although I certainly appreciate that."

She blew out a breath, not daring to look at him, before continuing. "I need you to support me, to argue with me, to care about me—but to let me make my own decisions. Which includes making my own mistakes. And then I need you to help me fix any problems I might have caused." Now she did look at him. "And I will do the same thing for you. You made a mistake. And together we did our best to fix it. And we did. *Together.*"

She sighed. "I need you to tell me what you want because I love you, and I need to know if I fit into your future." She looked away. "And don't blame Chal for anything. He had no idea I couldn't swim. All Chal did was not pay attention while I made a mistake."

"I know," Reo said. "I'll apologize to him before we leave." He sat down on the edge of the bed. "Maybe then he'll give us both a tour of Yeend." He leaned close. "I love you. I always have, but—"

"But what?" she interrupted. "Tell me what you want."

"You," he said. "Almost from the first moment I saw you." He sighed, but it was a sound of contentment. "And I promise I will do my best—"

Kara silenced him by pressing her mouth to his. He responded by sinking into her and wrapping a hand in her hair. She felt him smile and she pulled away.

"Your best is all I need," she said. "I have strict orders to stay in bed. Have any ideas?"

"I'm in trouble with you if I say no," Reo replied. "And in trouble with your healer if I say yes." He grinned and lay down beside her. "I have chosen my side."

He nuzzled her hair, trailing kisses along her neck.

"And what I want for my life." He leaned away from her and sighed. "I've always been too afraid to hope for, too afraid to say it out loud. But I want a life with you. Anywhere you decide. Here in Seyoya, away from Mage Guild and your mother, or on Old Rillidi. Wherever you are, that's where I want to be."

"Good." She smiled. "Because right now you're in my bed. And that's exactly where I want to be, with you."

She leaned up and kissed him, her tongue snaking into his mouth. Heat—their heat—coursed through her. He pushed the sheet down and pulled her thin shift over her head. She felt air on her skin, and then he leaned down and sucked one nipple into his mouth. She let out a shaky breath.

"No fair," she said. "You have way too many clothes on." She laughed when he shrugged out of his shirt and tossed it away, then ran her hands down his back, enjoying how his muscles bunched and lengthened as he leaned over her.

"Much better," she sighed as she felt his skin on hers, the heat between them growing where their skin met at chest and lips. She rubbed his back, her hands ending up at the waist of his trousers. She tugged at them and felt him smile against her lips as his hands left her shoulders. His hands pushed his trousers down and out of the way, then he slipped under the sheet and his hand moved to part her thighs.

She ran her hands across his buttocks as he moved between her legs, and once he was positioned, she both pushed him and drew him inside of her.

He kissed her again and then he raised his head, meeting her eyes as he rocked into her. The heat between them continued to rise, their urgency building. With a cry, she buried her head on his shoulder as waves of pleasure surged through her. With one last thrust, he exhaled, then relaxed onto her.

More hot kisses trailed down her neck, then Reo gathered her to him and drew the forgotten sheet over their now cooling bodies.

"SO THAT'S IT for another month?" Kara asked as Santos helped her from the boat. This was her second time clearing spells from Warrior Guild Hall since she and Reo had returned from Seyoya.

"Not enough of a challenge?" Santos asked.

Reo stepped onto the dock beside her and tied the little boat up before joining them. Unconsciously, she held her hand out to him and he grasped it.

"There didn't seem to be a lot of new attacks," Kara said. Her battle with the runaway mage mist had forced her skills to develop. Last month it had been so much easier to identify spells that were meant to do harm. "And the new ones were all from Rorik."

Santos sighed. "Probably because of some news I received earlier. I didn't want to distract you from this task but Arabella Fonti has given birth to a son."

Kara closed her eyes. The child of the man she'd killed. "I have another brother." She opened her eyes and set her mouth. "I want to see him. Santos, please tell Mage Guild that I want to see my brother."

"I thought you would say that," Santos replied. "I'll make sure your mother and Rorik know." He paused. "I think that's enough for today. I'll see you tomorrow morning for lessons." He turned and headed towards the manor house.

"Are you all right?" Reo asked her. He squeezed her hand.

"I will be," Kara replied. "It's not as though this was a surprise."

"Unlike all of the other surprises you've had to deal with." He smiled to soften his words. "Are you going to our cabin?"

"Now that Santos has said he doesn't need me for anything, yes." Our cabin: Kara still loved it when he said that. When they'd returned from Seyoya, Reo had moved his things into the cabin that they now shared, but he'd been slower to name it *their* place, instead calling it hers.

"I have some things to take care of," Reo said. "I'll meet you there later. Unless you don't want to be alone?"

"You go," she said. He kissed her, and she watched him as he followed the path that led to the manor house.

Besides, she wasn't alone. She had a family: people she loved and cared for who returned that love and care. She had a place in the world: a home. Finally.

She slowly started to walk towards the cabin Santos had built for his love: the cabin that she was privileged enough to share with hers: Reo.

About the Author

Jane Glatt loves that along with creating original worlds, writing fantasy allows her to indulge her curiosity about an eclectic group of subjects. So far she's researched synaesthesia, medieval guilds, tidal rivers, cities atop bridges, pirates and privateers, plants used for healing and the history of spying. For that last one she blames a visit to the International Spy Museum (yes it's a real place), in Washington D.C.

For news on Jane's future releases visit her website http://janeglatt.com/index.html and sign up for her newsletter.